D1325936

A Vintage Christmas

VINTAGE

CONTENTS

'Carol-Barking' from *Cider With Rosie*
by Laurie Lee

Laurie Lee was born in Stroud, Gloucestershire, in 1914, and was educated at Slad village school and Stroud Central School. At the age of nineteen he walked to London and then travelled on foot through Spain, where he was trapped by the outbreak of the Civil War. He later returned by crossing the Pyrenees, as described in his book *As I Walked Out One Midsummer Morning*. In 1950 he married Catherine Polge and they had one daughter. Laurie Lee died in May 1997. *Cider With Rosie* is Lee's memoir of childhood in the remote Cotswold village where he grew up. It is a vivid, enchanting evocation of a world that is both immediate and real but also belongs to a now-distant past.

Read more by Laurie Lee:
Cider With Rosie
A Rose for Winter

Later, towards Christmas, there was heavy snow, which raised the roads to the top of the hedges. There were millions of tons of the lovely stuff, plastic, pure, all-purpose, which nobody owned, which one could carve or tunnel, eat, or just throw about. It covered the hills and cut off the villages, but nobody thought of rescues; for there was hay in the barns and flour in the kitchens, the women baked bread, the cattle were fed and sheltered – we'd been cut off before, after all.

The week before Christmas, when snow seemed to lie thickest, was the moment for carol-singing; and when I think back to those nights it is to the crunch of snow and to the lights of the lanterns on it. Carol-singing in my village was a special tithe for the boys, the girls had little to do with it. Like hay-making, blackberrying, stone-clearing, and wishing-people-a-happy-Easter, it was one of our seasonal perks.

By instinct we knew just when to begin it; a day too soon and we should have been unwelcome, a day too late and we should have received lean looks from people whose bounty was already exhausted. When the true moment came, exactly balanced, we recognised it and were ready.

So as soon as the wood had been stacked in the oven to dry for the morning fire, we put on our scarves and went out through the streets, calling loudly between our hands, till the various boys who knew the signal ran out from their houses to join us.

One by one they came stumbling over the snow, swinging their lanterns around their heads, shouting and coughing horribly.

'Coming carol-barking then?'

We were the Church Choir, so no answer was necessary. For a year we had praised the Lord out of key, and as a reward for this service – on top of the Outing – we now had the right to visit all the big houses, to sing our carols and collect our tribute.

To work them all in meant a five-mile foot journey over wild and generally snowed-up country. So the first thing we did was to plan our route; a formality, as the route never changed. All the same, we blew on our fingers and argued; and then we chose our Leader. This was not binding, for we all fancied ourselves as Leaders, and he who started the night in that position usually trailed home with a bloody nose.

Eight of us set out that night. There was Sixpence the Tanner, who had never sung in his life (he just worked his mouth in church); the brothers Horace and Boney, who were always fighting everybody and always getting the worst of it; Clergy Green, the preaching maniac; Walt the bully, and my two brothers. As we went down the lane other boys, from other villages, were already about the hills, bawling 'Kingwenslush', and shouting through keyholes 'Knock on the knocker! Ring at the Bell! Give us a penny for singing so well!' They weren't an approved charity as we were, the Choir; but competition was in the air.

Our first call as usual was the house of the Squire, and we trouped nervously down his drive. For light we had candles in marmalade-jars suspended on loops of string, and they threw pale gleams on the towering snowdrifts that stood on each side of the drive. A blizzard was blowing, but we were well wrapped up, with Army puttees on our legs, woollen hats on our heads, and several scarves around our ears.

As we approached the Big House across its white silent lawns, we too grew respectfully silent. The lake near by was stiff and black, the waterfall frozen and still. We arranged ourselves shuffling around the big front door, then knocked and announced the Choir.

A maid bore the tidings of our arrival away into the echoing distances of the house, and while we waited we cleared our throats noisily. Then she came back, and the door was left ajar for us, and we were bidden to begin. We brought no music, the carols were in our heads. 'Let's give 'em "Wild Shepherds",' said Jack. We began in confusion, plunging into a wreckage of keys, of different words and tempo; but we gathered our strength; he who sang loudest took the rest of us with him, and the carol took shape if not sweetness.

This huge stone house, with its ivied walls, was always a mystery to us. What were those gables, those rooms and attics, those narrow windows veiled by the cedar trees. As we sang 'Wild Shepherds' we craned our necks, gaping into that lamplit hall which we had never entered; staring at the muskets and untenanted chairs, the great tapestries furred by dust – until suddenly, on the stairs, we saw the old Squire himself standing and listening with his head on one side.

He didn't move until we'd finished; then slowly he tottered towards us, dropped two coins in our box with a trembling hand, scratched his name in the book we carried, gave us each a long look with his moist blind eyes, then turned away in silence.

As though released from a spell, we took a few sedate steps, then broke into a run for the gate. We didn't stop till we were out of the grounds. Impatient, at last, to discover the extent of his bounty, we squatted by the cowsheds, held our lanterns over the book, and saw that he had written 'Two Shillings'. This was quite a good start. No one of any worth in the district would dare to give us less than the Squire.

So with money in the box, we pushed on up the valley, pouring scorn on each other's performance. Confident now, we began to consider our quality and whether one carol was not better suited to us than another. Horace,

Walt said, shouldn't sing at all; his voice was beginning to break. Horace disputed this and there was a brief token battle – they fought as they walked, kicking up divots of snow, then they forgot it, and Horace still sang.

Steadily we worked through the length of the valley, going from house to house, visiting the lesser and the greater gentry – the farmers, the doctors, the merchants, the majors, and other exalted persons. It was freezing hard and blowing too; yet not for a moment did we feel the cold. The snow blew into our faces, into our eyes and mouths, soaked through our puttees, got into our boots, and dripped from our woollen caps. But we did not care. The collecting-box grew heavier, and the list of names in the book longer and more extravagant, each trying to outdo the other.

Mile after mile we went, fighting against the wind, falling into snowdrifts, and navigating by the lights of the houses. And yet we never saw our audience. We called at house after house; we sang in courtyards and porches, outside windows, or in the damp gloom of hallways; we heard voices from hidden rooms; we smelt rich clothes and strange hot food; we saw maids bearing in dishes or carrying away coffee-cups; we received nuts, cakes, figs, preserved ginger, dates, cough-drops, and money; but we never once saw our patrons. We sang as it were at the castle walls, and apart from the Squire, who had shown himself to prove that he was still alive, we never expected it otherwise.

As the night drew on there was trouble with Boney. 'Noël', for instance, had a rousing harmony which Boney persisted in singing, and singing flat. The others forbade him to sing it at all, and Boney said he would fight us. Picking himself up, he agreed we were right, then he disappeared altogether. He just turned away and walked into the snow and wouldn't answer when we called him back. Much later, as we reached a far point up the valley, somebody said 'Hark!' and we stopped to listen. Far away across the fields from the distant village came the sound of a frail voice singing, singing 'Noël', and singing it flat – it was Boney, branching out on his own.

We approached our last house high up on the hill, the place of Joseph the farmer. For him we had chosen a special carol, which was about the other Joseph, so that we always felt that singing it added a spicy cheek to the night. The last stretch of country to reach his farm was perhaps the most difficult of all. In these rough bare lanes, open to all winds, sheep were buried and wagons lost. Huddled together, we tramped in one another's footsteps, powdered snow blew into our screwed-up eyes, the candles burnt low, some blew out altogether, and we talked loudly above the gale.

Crossing, at last, the frozen mill-stream – whose wheel in summer still turned a barren mechanism – we climbed up to Joseph's farm. Sheltered by trees, warm on its bed of snow, it seemed always to be like this. As always it was late; as always this was our final call. The snow had a fine crust upon it, and the old trees sparkled like tinsel.

We grouped ourselves round the farmhouse porch. The sky cleared, and broad streams of stars ran down over the valley and away to Wales. On Slad's white slopes, seen through the black sticks of its woods, some red lamps still burned in the windows.

Everything was quiet; everywhere there was the faint crackling silence of the winter night. We started singing, and we were all moved by the words and the sudden true-ness of our voices. Pure, very clear, and breathless we sang:

> 'As Joseph was a walking
> He heard an angel sing;
> "This night shall be the birth-time
> Of Christ the Heavenly King.
>
> He neither shall be bornèd
> In Housen nor in hall,
> Nor in a place of paradise
> But in an ox's stall . . ."

And two thousand Christmases became real to us then; the houses, the halls, the places of paradise had all been visited; the stars were bright to guide the Kings through the snow; and across the farmyard we could hear the beasts in their stalls. We were given roast apples and hot mince-pies, in our nostrils were spices like myrrh, and in our wooden box, as we headed back for the village, there were golden gifts for all.

'Obadiah Oak, Mrs Griffiths and the Carol Singers'
by Louis de Bernières

Louis de Bernières is the bestselling author of *Captain Corelli's Mandolin*, which won the Commonwealth Writers' Prize, Best Book in 1995. His most recent books are *The Dust That Falls From Dreams*, *Birds Without Wings* and *A Partisan's Daughter*, a collection of stories, *Notwithstanding*, and two collections of poetry, *Imagining Alexandria* and *Of Love and Desire*.

Read more by Louis de Bernières:
Captain Corelli's Mandolin
The Dust That Falls from Dreams
So Much Life Left Over

Mrs Griffiths goes to the shop and stands next to Obadiah Oak, her nose wrinkled in distaste. Obadiah, known
to all as Jack, lives with his daughter by the cricket green,
in a cottage that has been handed down in his family for
seven generations. Jack is the village's last peasant, and
he and his house smell of two hundred years of peasant
life; he exudes the aromas of wet leather and horse
manure, costive dogs, turnips, rainwater and cabbage
water, sausages, verdigris, woollen socks, Leicester
cheese, fish guts, fraying curtains, mice under the stairs,
mud on the carpet and woodlice behind the pipes, but
most of all he reeks of six decades of neglected hygiene.
Jack is considered a 'character', with his teeth like
tombstones, his stubble like a filecard, his lips like kip-
pers, his rolling Surrey accent and his eyes as round as
plates, but newcomers avoid him if they can. They moved
here in search of picture-postcard England, and are

uncomfortable with a real countryman who knows how
to wring the neck of a chicken and has no compunction
about drowning kittens in a bucket. Jack is an anachron-
ism, but he does not know it, and he is standing in the
village shop because he has nothing to do, and not many
to talk with. Every day he comes in and buys cigarette
papers, so that by now he must have a roomful of them,
and he engages the shop assistant in a dilatory conversation about the weather, punctuating his remarks with
hawking. He used to spit it out, but nowadays he swal-
lows it, having been roundly told off one afternoon by the
squirrel-shooting Polly Wantage.

'Artnoon,' he says to Mrs Griffiths. 'Turned out nice
again. Looks like rain though.'

'Getting chilly,' replies Mrs Griffiths crisply, hoping to
avoid a prolonged conversation.

'Time o' year,' says Jack, 'what wi' Christmas on the
doorstep. Going away?'

'Staying at home. I usually do.'

'Come and eat wi' us?' says Jack, knowing that she will
refuse, because everyone always does. He does not in
truth want to have Mrs Griffiths round for Christmas dinner, but he has always been the kind of man who tries to
do his bit, the sort of fellow who will offer his sturdy back
to a child who wants to climb a tree to fetch down
conkers.

'Oh, I couldn't possibly,' says Mrs Griffiths shortly,
without even thanking him. But Jack is not offended; he

has a sense of his place in the world, and a sensible man expects snooty people to be snooty.

'Happy Christmas, then,' he says, and he touches the rim of his sagging hat. He leaves the shop and strolls home, directly across the middle of the cricket pitch. He has been asked not to, but cannot see the point of being tender in the winter about a pitch that is mangled every weekend of the summer.

Mrs Griffiths exchanges resigned glances with Mrs Davidson, whose turn it is to man the shop. It makes no profit any more; no one would buy it from the previous owner, and now it is run on a cooperative and voluntary basis by those ladies who have time on their hands.

'I don't know why someone doesn't tell that man to wash,' says Mrs Griffiths, crossly. 'It's a disgrace.'

'Oh, I know,' says Mrs Davidson. 'Polly Wantage told him once, you know, after she stopped him from spitting, and what he said to her was unrepeatable.'

Mrs Griffiths' eyes widen with a kind of horrified delight. Strong language is so far outside her world that when she overhears it, it is as exotic as Bengal tigers.

Mrs Griffiths buys a big box of Christmas cards because she wants Mrs Davidson to think that she has lots of friends and relations. She will send a card to the vicar and the doctor, and she will drop one through the letter boxes of the more respectable people in the village, so that they will send one back, and then, should anyone call round and glance at her cards, it will be clear that she is well connected and respected. She also buys mincemeat and ready-made frozen shortcrust pastry, because tonight she is going to make mince pies for the carol singers.

Mrs Griffiths has always hated the carol singers, even though they are the children of the better families. They arrives with their guitars and their recorders, and every year they sing the same two songs, 'Silent Night' and 'O Come All Ye Faithful'. They collect for the NSPCC, and Mrs Griffiths would really rather give money to the RSPCA; at least animals cannot be blamed for anything, and do not grow up to be thieves and yobs. Mrs Griffiths secretly resents the way in which the carol singers are so young and bright-eyed, so full of high laughter, so full of the future, and previously she has always turned out the lights when she heard them coming, so that she does not have to go out and listen to them, or give them money, or make mince pies and hot punch as everyone else does. The carol singers have always sung to her closed door and doused lights, and have then departed.

But things have changed. Mrs Griffiths lost her husband in the spring, and is slowly realising that at last the time has come when she has to make an effort to get on with people. She did not love her husband, he was boring and inconsequential, and she had not even loved him when they married. After he died, she felt merely a sense of relief, conjoined with the bitterness of a freedom that has come too late. Sometimes she wonders whether she has ever loved anyone at all, and certainly she has never loved anyone as they do on the television late at night, with all those heaving backsides. But, even though her husband was a cipher, nowadays Mrs Griffiths feels a certain emptiness, a certain need to reach out, a certain need to be reborn. Tonight she will make mince pies and punch, she will leave the lights on, she will come out and listen, and she will tell the children that their music is wonderful. She will ignore the fact that they know only one verse of 'Silent Night', their guitars are out of tune and their recorders too shrill, and she will wish them a happy Christmas even though they are beautiful and still have a chance in life.

Mrs Griffiths covers herself and her kitchen in dusting sugar, she deals with the frustration of pastry that sticks to the table and the rolling pin, she conquers the meanness that nearly prevents her from pouring a whole bottle of red wine into the punch, and then she waits, sitting on the wooden chair in the kitchen, warmed by the rich smells of baking pastry and hot wine, and lemon, and rum. 'After they've been,' she thinks, 'I will write all my cards, and then I'll draw a hot bath and read.' Since her husband died, Mrs Griffiths has taken to reading true-life romances that one can order six at a time from a special club. She has read so many that she thinks she could probably write one herself.

It grows very dark, and three hours pass. Mrs Griffiths goes often to her door, and opens it, to see if she can hear the carol singers coming. The night is very cold; there is a frosty wind, but she does not think that it is going to rain. They will be here before long.

Mrs Griffiths sits in her wooden chair and thinks about what she should say to the children; does 'Merry Christmas' sound better than 'Happy Christmas'? Does 'Thank you so much for coming' sound too formal? The young are not very formal these days. During the time when everyone was going on about the Beatles, the youngsters kept saying 'groovy', but that was probably not very 'with it' any more. She is not even sure if 'with it' is 'with it' these days. She experiments with 'Groovy Christmas', but decides against it.

Mrs Griffiths hears 'Silent Night' in the distance. The children are singing to the gypsies in their scrapyard, causing the Alsatians to howl. Now they are singing to the Davidsons, and now they are singing to the baroque musicologist, and now they are singing to smelly Jack Oak. Mrs Griffiths listens very hard for the squeak of her garden gate and the experimental chords of the guitarists. She knows that, in between the houses, the children bray out songs from pop groups with silly names and working-class accents.

The children arrive at the garden gate, and the tall, lanky one says, 'What about this one?'

'Not worth it,' says the other guitarist, who is proud of the fact that he is going to get a shaving kit for Christmas. He strokes his invisible moustache with a nail-bitten forefinger.

'She's an old skinflint,' says the blonde girl who will be beautiful when she loses her puppy fat.

'Her husband died,' says the dark, sensitive girl with the brown eyes.

'It won't do any harm, will it?' asks the blonde girl.

'There's no point,' says the lanky boy, 'she just turns off the lights as soon as she hears us coming. Every year it's the same, don't you remember? She's an old ratbag.'

'Mum told us not to leave her out,' says the blonde.

'Who's going to tell Mum?' demands her brother. 'Let's go and do the Armstrongs.'

Mrs Griffiths sits on her wooden chair and hears 'Silent Night' coming from next door. At first she feels a livid pang of anger, and one or two of those vehement forbidden words spring to her mind, but not to her lips. She is indignant, and thinks, 'How dare they miss me out. They always come here. Why am I the one to miss out?' She looks at her inviting heap of mince pies and her steaming bowl of punch, and thinks, 'I did all this for them.' She wants to go outside and shout insults at them, but she cannot think of anything that would not sound ridiculous and undignified.

Alongside her anger and frustration, Mrs Griffiths abruptly feels more tired and forlorn than she has ever felt in her life, and she begins to cry for the first time since she was a child. She is surprised by large tears that well up in her eyes and slide down the sides of her nose, rolling down her hands and wrists, and into her sleeves.

She had not remembered that tears could be so warm. She tastes one, in order to be reminded of their saltiness, and finds it comforting. She thinks, 'Perhaps I should get a cat,' and fetches some kitchen roll so that she can blow her nose.

Mrs Griffiths begins to write her cards. One for the vicar, one for the doctor, one for the people in the mansion, one for the Conservative councillor. She gets up from her chair and, without really thinking about it, eats a mince pie and takes a glass of punch. She had forgotten how good they can be, and she feels the punch igniting her insides. The sensuality of it shocks and seduces her, and she takes another glass.

Mrs Griffiths cries some more, but this time it is partly for pleasure, for the pleasure of the hot briny water, and the sheer self-indulgence. A rebellious whim creeps up on her. She glances around as if to check that she is truly alone in the house, and then she stands up and shouts, 'Bloody bloody bloody bloody bloody.' She adds, 'Bloody children, bloody bloody.' She attempts 'bollocks' but merely embarrasses herself and tries 'bugger' instead. She drinks more punch and says, 'Bloody bugger.' She writes a card to the gypsies who own the scrapyard, and to the water-board man who had an illegitimate child by a Swedish barmaid, and to the people who own the pub and vote Labour. She eats two mince pies at once, cramming them into her mouth, one on top of the other, and the crumbs and the sugar settle on to the front of her cardigan. She fetches a biscuit tin, and puts into it six of the remaining pies. She presses down the lid and ventures out into the night.

When she returns she finishes off the punch, and then heaves herself upstairs with the aid of the banisters.

She is beginning to feel distinctly ill, and heads for her bed with the unconscious but unswerving instinct of a homing pigeon. She reminds herself to draw the curtains so that no one will be able to pry and spy, and then she undresses with difficulty, and throws her clothes on to the floor with all the perverse but justified devilment of one who has been brought up not to, and has never tried it before. She extinguishes the light and crawls into bed, but every time that she closes her eyes she begins to feel seasick. Her eyes glitter in the dark like those of a small girl, the years are briefly annulled, and she remembers how to feel frightened when an owl hoots outside.

At eleven thirty, fetid Jack Oak opens his front door to put the cat out and spots a biscuit tin by the door scraper. He picks it up, curious, and takes it back inside. 'Look what some'un left,' he says to his daughter, who is just as unkempt as he is, but smells more sweetly.

'Well, open it,' she says.

Jack prises off the lid with his thick yellow nails, and inside he finds six mince pies, and an envelope. Jack almost never gets Christmas cards. He feels a leap of excitement and pleasure in his belly, and hands the card to his daughter to read. It says: *'To dear Mr Obadiah Oak and daughter, a very Happy Christmas and New Year, from Marjorie Griffiths.'*

'Well, bugger me,' says Jack, and his daughter says, 'Now there's a turn-up for the books.' Jack puts the card on the mantelpiece, crams a whole mince pie into his mouth, and delves among the clutter for a pencil and the box of yellowing cards that he bought from the village shop fifteen years ago.

'The Turkey Season'
by Alice Munro

Alice Munro was born in 1931 and is the author of thirteen collections of stories. She has received many awards and prizes, including three of Canada's Governor General's Literary Awards and two Giller Prizes, the Rea Award for the Short Story, the Lannan Literary Award, the WHSmith Book Award in the UK, the National Book Critics Circle Award in the US, was shortlisted for the Booker Prize for *The Beggar Maid*, and has been awarded the Man Booker International Prize 2009 for her overall contribution to fiction on the world stage, and in 2013 she won the Nobel Prize in Literature. She lives with her husband in Clinton, Ontario, near Lake Huron in Canada.

Read more by Alice Munro:

Dear Life

Runaway

Hateship, Friendship, Courtship, Loveship, Marriage

TO JOE RADFORD

When I was fourteen I got a job at the Turkey Barn for the Christmas season. I was still too young to get a job working in a store or as a part-time waitress; I was also too nervous.

I was a turkey gutter. The other people who worked at the Turkey Barn were Lily and Marjorie and Gladys, who were also gutters; Irene and Henry, who were pluckers; Herb Abbott, the foreman, who superintended the whole operation and filled in wherever he was needed. Morgan Elliott was the owner and boss. He and his son, Morgy, did the killing.

Morgy I knew from school. I thought him stupid and despicable and was uneasy about having to consider him in a new and possibly superior guise, as the boss's son. But his father treated him so roughly, yelling and swearing at him, that he seemed no more than the lowest of the workers. The other person related to the boss was

Gladys. She was his sister, and in her case there did seem to be some privilege of position. She worked slowly and went home if she was not feeling well, and was not friendly to Lily and Marjorie, although she was, a little, to me. She had come back to live with Morgan and his family after working for many years in Toronto, in a bank. This was not the sort of job she was used to. Lily and Marjorie, talking about her when she wasn't there, said she had had a nervous breakdown. They said Morgan made her work in the Turkey Barn to pay for her keep. They also said, with no worry about the contradiction, that she had taken the job because she was after a man, and that the man was Herb Abbott.

All I could see when I closed my eyes, the first few nights after working there, was turkeys. I saw them hanging upside down, plucked and stiffened, pale and cold, with the heads and necks limp, the eyes and nostrils clotted with dark blood; the remaining bits of feathers – those dark and bloody too – seemed to form a crown. I saw them not with aversion but with a sense of endless work to be done.

Herb Abbott showed me what to do. You put the turkey down on the table and cut its head off with a cleaver. Then you took the loose skin around the neck and stripped it back to reveal the crop, nestled in the cleft between the gullet and the windpipe.

'Feel the gravel,' said Herb encouragingly. He made me close my fingers around the crop. Then he showed me how to work my hand down behind it to cut it out, and the gullet and windpipe as well. He used shears to cut the vertebrae.

'Scrunch, scrunch,' he said soothingly. 'Now, put your hand in.'

I did. It was deathly cold in there, in the turkey's dark insides.

'Watch out for bone splinters.'

Working cautiously in the dark, I had to pull the connecting tissues loose.

'Ups-a-daisy.' Herb turned the bird over and flexed each leg. 'Knees up, Mother Brown. Now.' He took a heavy knife and placed it directly on the knee knuckle joints and cut off the shank.

'Have a look at the worms.'

Pearly-white strings, pulled out of the shank, were creeping about on their own.

'That's just the tendons shrinking. Now comes the nice part!'

He slit the bird at its bottom end, letting out a rotten smell.

'Are you educated?'

I did not know what to say.

'What's that smell?'

'Hydrogen sulfide.'

'Educated,' said Herb, sighing. 'All right. Work your fingers around and get the guts loose. Easy. Easy. Keep your fingers together. Keep the palm inwards. Feel the ribs with the back of your hand. Feel the guts fit into your palm. Feel that? Keep going. Break the strings – as many as you can. Keep going. Feel a hard lump? That's the gizzard. Feel a soft lump? That's the heart. Okay? Okay. Get your fingers around the gizzard. Easy. Start pulling this way. That's right. That's right. Start to pull her out.'

It was not easy at all. I wasn't even sure what I had was the gizzard. My hand was full of cold pulp.

'Pull,' he said, and I brought out a glistening, liverish mass.

'Got it. There's the lights. You know what they are? Lungs. There's the heart. There's the gizzard. There's the gall. Now, you don't ever want to break that gall inside or it will taste the entire turkey.' Tactfully, he scraped out what I had missed, including the testicles, which were like a pair of white grapes.

'Nice pair of earrings,' Herb said.

Herb Abbott was a tall, firm, plump man. His hair was dark and thin, combed straight back from a widow's peak, and his eyes seemed to be slightly slanted, so that he looked like a pale Chinese or like pictures of the Devil, except that he was smooth-faced and benign. Whatever he did around the Turkey Barn – gutting, as he was now, or loading the truck, or hanging the carcasses – was done with efficient, economical movements, quickly and buoyantly. 'Notice about Herb – he always walks like he had a boat moving underneath him,' Marjorie said, and it was true. Herb worked on the lake boats, during the season, as a cook. Then he worked for Morgan until after Christmas.

The rest of the time he helped around the poolroom, making hamburgers, sweeping up, stopping fights before they got started. That was where he lived: he had a room above the poolroom on the main street.

In all the operations at the Turkey Barn it seemed to be Herb who had the efficiency and honor of the business continually on his mind; it was he who kept everything under control. Seeing him in the yard talking to Morgan, who was a thick, short man, red in the face, an unpredictable bully, you would be sure that it was Herb who was the boss and Morgan the hired help. But it was not so.

If I had not had Herb to show me, I don't think I could have learned turkey gutting at all. I was clumsy with my hands and had been shamed for it so often that the least show of impatience on the part of the person instructing me could have brought on a dithering paralysis. I could not stand to be watched by anybody but Herb. Particularly, I couldn't stand to be watched by Lily and Marjorie, two middle-aged sisters, who were very fast and thorough and competitive gutters. They sang at their work and talked abusively and intimately to the turkey carcasses.

'Don't you nick me, you old bugger!'

'Aren't you the old crap factory!'

I had never heard women talk like that.

Gladys was not a fast gutter, though she must have been thorough; Herb would have talked to her otherwise. She never sang and certainly she never swore. I thought her rather old, though she was not as old as Lily and

Marjorie; she must have been over thirty. She seemed offended by everything that went on and had the air of keeping plenty of bitter judgments to herself. I never tried to talk to her, but she spoke to me one day in the cold little washroom off the gutting shed. She was putting pancake makeup on her face. The color of the makeup was so distinct from the color of her skin that it was as if she were slapping orange paint over a whitewashed, bumpy wall.

She asked me if my hair was naturally curly.

I said yes.

'You don't have to get a permanent?'

'No.'

'You're lucky. I have to do mine up every night. The chemicals in my system won't allow me to get a permanent.'

There are different ways women have of talking about their looks. Some women make it clear that what they do to keep themselves up is for the sake of sex, for men. Others, like Gladys, make the job out to be a kind of housekeeping, whose very difficulties they pride themselves on. Gladys was genteel. I could see her in the bank, in a navy-blue dress with the kind of detachable white collar you can wash at night. She would be grumpy and correct.

Another time, she spoke to me about her periods, which were profuse and painful. She wanted to know about mine. There was an uneasy, prudish, agitated expression on her face. I was saved by Irene, who was using the toilet and called out, 'Do like me, and you'll be rid of all your problems for a while.' Irene was only a few years older than I was, but she was recently – tardily – married, and heavily pregnant.

Gladys ignored her, running cold water on her hands. The hands of all of us were red and sore-looking from the work. 'I can't use that soap. If I use it, I break out in a rash,' Gladys said. 'If I bring my own soap in here, I can't afford to have other people using it, because I pay a lot for it – it's a special anti-allergy soap.'

I think the idea that Lily and Marjorie promoted – that Gladys was after Herb Abbott – sprang from their belief that single people ought to be teased and embarrassed whenever possible, and from their interest in Herb, which led to the feeling that somebody ought to be after him. They wondered about him. What they wondered was, How can a man want so little? No wife, no family, no house. The details of his daily life, the small preferences, were of interest. Where had he been brought up? (Here and there and all over.) How far had he gone in school? (Far enough.) Where was his girlfriend? (Never tell.) Did he drink coffee or tea if he got the choice? (Coffee.)

When they talked about Gladys's being after him they must have really wanted to talk about sex – what he wanted and what he got. They must have felt a voluptuous curiosity about him, as I did. He aroused this feeling by being circumspect and not making the jokes some men did, and at the same time by not being squeamish or gentlemanly. Some men, showing me the testicles from the turkey, would have acted as if the very existence of testicles were somehow a bad joke on me, something a girl could be taunted about; another sort of man would have been embarrassed and would have thought he had to protect me from embarrassment. A man who didn't seem to feel one way or the other was an oddity – as much to older women, probably, as to me. But what was so welcome to me may have been disturbing to them. They wanted to jolt him. They even wanted Gladys to jolt him, if she could.

There wasn't any idea then – at least in Logan, Ontario, in the late forties – about homosexuality's going beyond very narrow confines. Women, certainly, believed in its rarity and in definite boundaries. There were homosexuals in town, and we knew who they were: an elegant, light-voiced, wavy-haired paperhanger who called himself an interior decorator; the minister's widow's fat, spoiled only son, who went so far as to enter baking contests and had crocheted a tablecloth; a hypochondriacal church organist and music teacher who kept the choir and his pupils in line with screaming tantrums. Once the label was fixed, there was a good deal of tolerance for these people, and their talents for decorating, for crocheting, and for music were appreciated – especially by women. 'The poor fellow,' they said. 'He doesn't do any harm.' They really seemed to believe – the women did – that it was the penchant for baking or music that was the determining factor, and that it was this activity that made the man what he was – not any other detours he might take, or wish to take.

A desire to play the violin would be taken as more a deviation from manliness than would a wish to shun women. Indeed, the idea was that any manly man would wish to shun women but most of them were caught off guard, and for good.

I don't want to go into the question of whether Herb was homosexual or not, because the definition is of no use to me. I think that probably he was, but maybe he was not. (Even considering what happened later, I think that.) He is not a puzzle so arbitrarily solved.

The other plucker, who worked with Irene, was Henry Streets, a neighbor of ours. There was nothing remarkable about him except that he was eighty-six years old and still, as he said of himself, a devil for work. He had whisky in his thermos, and drank it from time to time through the day. It was Henry who said to me, in our kitchen, 'You ought to get yourself a job at the Turkey Barn. They need another gutter.' Then my father said at once, 'Not her, Henry. She's got ten thumbs,' and Henry said he was just joking – it was dirty work. But I was already determined to try it – I had a great need to be successful in a job like that. I was almost in the condition of a grown-up person who is ashamed of never having learned to read, so much did I feel my ineptness at manual work. Work, to everybody I knew, meant doing things I was no good at doing, and work was what people prided themselves on and measured each other by. (It goes without saying that the

things I was good at, like schoolwork, were suspect or
held in plain contempt.) So it was a surprise and then a
triumph for me not to get fired, and to be able to turn out
clean turkeys at a rate that was not disgraceful. I don't
know if I really understood how much Herb Abbott was
responsible for this, but he would sometimes say, 'Good
girl,' or pat my waist and say, 'You're getting to be a good
gutter – you'll go a long ways in the world,' and when I felt
his quick, kind touch through the heavy sweater and
bloody smock I wore, I felt my face glow and I wanted to
lean back against him as he stood behind me. I wanted to
rest my head against his wide, fleshy shoulder. When I
went to sleep at night, lying on my side, I would run my
cheek against the pillow and think of that as Herb's
shoulder.

I was interested in how he talked to Gladys, how he
looked at her or noticed her. This interest was not jealousy.
I think I wanted something to happen with them. I quivered
in curious expectation, as Lily and Marjorie did. We all
wanted to see the flicker of sexuality in him, hear it in his
voice, not because we thought it would make him seem
more like other men but because we knew that with him it
would be entirely different. He was kinder and more patient
than most women, and as stern and remote, in some ways,
as any man. We wanted to see how he could be moved.

If Gladys wanted this too, she didn't give any signs of
it. It is impossible for me to tell with women like her
whether they are as thick and deadly as they seem, not

wanting anything much but opportunities for irritation and contempt, or if they are all choked up with gloomy fires and useless passions.

Marjorie and Lily talked about marriage. They did not have much good to say about it, in spite of their feeling that it was a state nobody should be allowed to stay out of. Marjorie said that shortly after her marriage she had gone into the woodshed with the intention of swallowing Paris green.

'I'd have done it,' she said. 'But the man came along in the grocery truck and I had to go out and buy the groceries. This was when we lived on the farm.'

Her husband was cruel to her in those days, but later he suffered an accident – he rolled the tractor and was so badly hurt he would be an invalid all his life. They moved to town, and Marjorie was the boss now.

'He starts to sulk the other night and say he don't want his supper. Well, I just picked up his wrist and held it. He was scared I was going to twist his arm. He could see I'd do it. So I say, "You *what*?" And he says, "I'll eat it."'

They talked about their father. He was a man of the old school. He had a noose in the woodshed (not the Paris green woodshed – this would be an earlier one, on another farm), and when they got on his nerves he used to line them up and threaten to hang them. Lily, who was the younger, would shake till she fell down. This same father had arranged to marry Marjorie off to a crony of his when she was just sixteen. That was the husband who had driven her to the Paris green. Their father did it because he wanted to be sure she wouldn't get into trouble.

'Hot blood,' Lily said.

I was horrified, and asked, 'Why didn't you run away?'

'His word was law,' Marjorie said.

They said that was what was the matter with kids nowadays – it was the kids that ruled the roost. A father's word should be law. They brought up their own kids strictly, and none had turned out bad yet. When Marjorie's son wet the bed she threatened to cut off his dingy with the butcher knife. That cured him.

They said ninety percent of the young girls nowadays drank, and swore, and took it lying down. They did not have daughters, but if they did and caught them at anything like that they would beat them raw. Irene, they said, used to go to the hockey games with her ski pants slit and nothing under them, for convenience in the snowdrifts afterward. Terrible.

I wanted to point out some contradictions. Marjorie and Lily themselves drank and swore, and what was so wonderful about the strong will of a father who would insure you a lifetime of unhappiness? (What I did not see was that Marjorie and Lily were not unhappy altogether – could not be, because of their sense of consequence, their pride and style.) I could be enraged then at the lack of logic in most adults' talk – the way they held to their pronouncements no matter what evidence might be presented to them. How could these women's hands be so gifted, so delicate and clever – for I knew they would be as good at dozens of other jobs as they were at gutting; they would be good at quilting and darning and painting and papering and kneading dough and setting out seedlings – and their thinking so slapdash, clumsy, infuriating?

Lily said she never let her husband come near her if he had been drinking. Marjorie said since the time she nearly died with a hemorrhage she never let her husband come near her, period. Lily said quickly that it was only when he'd been drinking that he tried anything. I could see that it was a matter of pride not to let your husband come near you, but I couldn't quite believe that 'come near' meant 'have sex'. The idea of Marjorie and Lily being sought out for such purposes seemed grotesque. They had bad teeth, their stomachs sagged, their faces were dull and spotty. I decided to take 'come near' literally.

The two weeks before Christmas was a frantic time at the Turkey Barn. I began to go in for an hour before school as well as after school and on weekends. In the morning, when I walked to work, the streetlights would still be on and the morning stars shining. There was the Turkey Barn, on the edge of a white field, with a row of big pine trees behind it, and always, no matter how cold and still it was, these trees were lifting their branches and sighing and straining. It seems unlikely that on my way to the Turkey Barn, for an hour of gutting turkeys, I should have experienced such a sense of promise and at the same time of perfect, impenetrable mystery in the universe, but I did. Herb had something to do with that, and so did the cold snap – the series of hard, clear mornings. The truth is, such feelings weren't hard to come by then. I would get them but not know how they were to be connected with anything in real life.

One morning at the Turkey Barn there was a new gutter. This was a boy eighteen or nineteen years old, a stranger named Brian. It seemed he was a relative, or perhaps just a friend, of Herb Abbott's. He was staying with Herb. He had worked on a lake boat last summer. He said he had got sick of it, though, and quit.

What he said was 'Yeah, fuckin' boats, I got sick of that.'

Language at the Turkey Barn was coarse and free, but this was one word never heard there. And Brian's use of it seemed not careless but flaunting, mixing insult and provocation. Perhaps it was his general style that made it so. He had amazing good looks: taffy hair, bright blue eyes, ruddy skin, well-shaped body – the sort of good looks nobody disagrees about for a moment. But a single, relentless notion had got such a hold on him that he could not keep from turning all his assets into parody. His mouth was wet-looking and slightly open most of the time, his eyes were half shut, his expression a hopeful leer, his movements indolent, exaggerated, inviting. Perhaps if he had been put on a stage with a microphone and a guitar and let grunt and howl and wriggle and excite, he would have seemed a true celebrant. Lacking a stage, he was unconvincing. After a while he seemed just like somebody with a bad case of hiccups – his insistent sexuality was that monotonous and meaningless.

If he had toned down a bit, Marjorie and Lily would probably have enjoyed him. They could have kept up a game of telling him to shut his filthy mouth and keep his hands to himself. As it was, they said they were sick of him, and meant it. Once, Marjorie took up her gutting knife. 'Keep your distance,' she said. 'I mean from me and my sister and that kid.'

She did not tell him to keep his distance from Gladys, because Gladys wasn't there at the time and Marjorie would probably not have felt like protecting her anyway. But it was Gladys Brian particularly liked to bother. She would throw down her knife and go into the washroom and stay there ten minutes and come out with a stony face. She didn't say she was sick any more and go home, the way she used to. Marjorie said Morgan was mad at Gladys for sponging and she couldn't get away with it any longer.

Gladys said to me, 'I can't stand that kind of thing. I can't stand people mentioning that kind of thing and that kind of – gestures. It makes me sick to my stomach.'

I believed her. She was terribly white. But why, in that case, did she not complain to Morgan? Perhaps relations between them were too uneasy, perhaps she could not bring herself to repeat or describe such things. Why did none of us complain – if not to Morgan, at least to Herb?

I never thought of it. Brian seemed just something to put up with, like the freezing cold in the gutting shed and the smell of blood and waste. When Marjorie and Lily did threaten to complain, it was about Brian's laziness.

He was not a good gutter. He said his hands were too big. So Herb took him off gutting, told him he was to sweep and clean up, make packages of giblets, and help load the truck. This meant that he did not have to be in any one place or doing any one job at a given time, so much of the time he did nothing. He would start sweeping up, leave that and mop the tables, leave that and have a cigarette, lounge against the table bothering us until Herb called him to help load. Herb was very busy now and spent a lot of time making deliveries, so it was possible he did not know the extent of Brian's idleness.

'I don't know why Herb don't fire you,' Marjorie said. 'I guess the answer is he don't want you hanging around sponging on him, with no place to go.'

'I know where to go,' said Brian.

'Keep your sloppy mouth shut,' said Marjorie. 'I pity Herb. Getting saddled.'

On the last school day before Christmas we got out early in the afternoon. I went home and changed my clothes and came in to work at about three o'clock. Nobody was working. Everybody was in the gutting shed, where Morgan Elliott was swinging a cleaver over the gutting table and yelling. I couldn't make out what the yelling was about, and thought someone must have made a terrible mistake in his work; perhaps it had been me. Then I saw Brian on the other side of the table, looking very sulky and mean, and standing well back. The sexual leer was not altogether gone from his face, but it was flattened out and mixed with a look of impotent bad temper and some fear. That's it, I thought, Brian is getting fired for being so sloppy and lazy. Even when I made out Morgan saying 'pervert' and 'filthy' and 'maniac', I still thought that was what was happening. Marjorie and Lily, and even brassy Irene, were standing around with downcast, rather pious looks, such as children get when somebody is suffering a terrible bawling out at school. Only old Henry seemed able to keep a cautious grin on his face. Gladys was not to be seen. Herb was standing closer to Morgan than anybody else. He was not interfering but was keeping an eye on the cleaver. Morgy was blubbering, though he didn't seem to be in any immediate danger.

Morgan was yelling at Brian to get out. 'And out of this town – I mean it – and don't you wait till tomorrow if you still want your arse in one piece! Out!' he shouted, and the cleaver swung dramatically towards the door. Brian started in that direction but, whether he meant to or not, he made a swaggering, taunting motion of the buttocks. This made Morgan break into a roar and run after him, swinging the cleaver in a stagy way. Brian ran, and Morgan ran after him, and Irene screamed and grabbed her stomach. Morgan was too heavy to run any distance and probably could not have thrown the cleaver very far, either. Herb watched from the doorway. Soon Morgan came back and flung the cleaver down on the table.

'All back to work! No more gawking around here! You don't get paid for gawking! What are you getting under way at?' he said, with a hard look at Irene.

'Nothing,' Irene said meekly.

'If you're getting under way get out of here.'

'I'm not.'

'All right, then!'

We got to work. Herb took off his blood-smeared smock and put on his jacket and went off, probably to see that Brian got ready to go on the suppertime bus. He did not say a word. Morgan and his son went out to the yard, and Irene and Henry went back to the adjoining shed, where they did the plucking, working knee-deep in the feathers Brian was supposed to keep swept up.

'Where's Gladys?' I said softly.

'Recuperating,' said Marjorie. She too spoke in a quieter voice than usual, and *recuperating* was not the sort of word she and Lily normally used. It was a word to be used about Gladys, with a mocking intent.

They didn't want to talk about what had happened, because they were afraid Morgan might come in and catch them at it and fire them. Good workers as they were, they were afraid of that. Besides, they hadn't seen anything. They must have been annoyed that they hadn't. All I ever found out was that Brian had either done something or shown something to Gladys as she came out of the washroom and she had started screaming and having hysterics.

Now she'll likely be laid up with another nervous breakdown, they said. And he'll be on his way out of town. And good riddance, they said, to both of them.

I have a picture of the Turkey Barn crew taken on Christmas Eve. It was taken with a flash camera that was someone's Christmas extravagance. I think it was Irene's. But Herb Abbott must have been the one who took the picture. He was the one who could be trusted to know or to learn immediately how to manage anything new, and flash cameras were fairly new at the time. The picture was taken about ten o'clock on Christmas Eve, after Herb and Morgy had come back from making the last delivery and we had washed off the gutting table and swept and mopped the cement floor. We had taken off our bloody smocks and heavy sweaters and gone into the little room called the lunchroom, where there was a table and a heater. We still wore our working clothes: overalls and shirts. The men wore caps and the women kerchiefs, tied in the wartime style. I am stout and cheerful and comradely in the picture, transformed into someone I don't ever remember being or pretending to be. I look years older than fourteen. Irene is the only one who has taken off her kerchief, freeing her long red hair. She peers out from it with a meek, sluttish, inviting look, which would match her reputation but is not like any look of hers I remember. Yes, it must have been her camera; she is posing for it, with that look, more deliberately than anyone else is. Marjorie and Lily are smiling, true to form, but their smiles are sour and reckless. With their hair hidden, and such figures as they have bundled up, they look like a couple of tough and jovial but testy workmen. Their kerchiefs look misplaced; caps would be better. Henry is in high spirits, glad to be part of the work force, grinning and looking twenty years younger than his age. Then Morgy, with his hangdog look, not trusting the occasion's bounty, and Morgan very flushed and bosslike and satisfied. He has just given each of us our bonus turkey. Each of these turkeys has a leg or a wing missing, or a malformation of some kind, so none of them are salable at the full price. But Morgan has been at pains to tell us that you often get the best meat off the gimpy ones, and he has shown us that he's taking one home himself.

We are all holding mugs or large, thick china cups, which contain not the usual tea but rye whisky. Morgan and Henry have been drinking since suppertime. Marjorie and Lily say they only want a little, and only take it at all because it's Christmas Eve and they are dead on their feet. Irene says she's dead on her feet as well but that doesn't mean she only wants a little. Herb has poured quite generously not just for her but for Lily and Marjorie too, and they do not object. He has measured mine and Morgy's out at the same time, very stingily, and poured in Coca-Cola.

This is the first drink I have ever had, and as a result I will believe for years that rye-and-Coca-Cola is a standard sort of drink and will always ask for it, until I notice that few other people drink it and that it makes me sick. I didn't get sick that Christmas Eve, though; Herb had not given me enough. Except for an odd taste, and my own feeling of consequence, it was like drinking Coca-Cola.

I don't need Herb in the picture to remember what he looked like. That is, if he looked like himself, as he did all the time at the Turkey Barn and the few times I saw him on the street – as he did all the times in my life when I saw him except one.

The time he looked somewhat unlike himself was when Morgan was cursing out Brian and, later, when Brian had run off down the road. What was this different look? I've tried to remember, because I studied it hard at the time. It wasn't much different. His face looked softer and heavier then, and if you had to describe the expression on it you would have to say it was an expression of shame. But what would he be ashamed of? Ashamed of Brian, for the way he had behaved? Surely that would be late in the day; when had Brian ever behaved otherwise? Ashamed of Morgan, for carrying on so ferociously and theatrically? Or of himself, because he was famous for nipping fights and displays of this sort in the bud and hadn't been able to do it here? Would he be ashamed that he hadn't stood up for Brian? Would he have expected himself to do that, to stand up for Brian?

All this was what I wondered at the time. Later, when I knew more, at least about sex, I decided that Brian was Herb's lover, and that Gladys really was trying to get attention from Herb, and that that was why Brian had humiliated her – with or without Herb's connivance and consent. Isn't it true that people like Herb – dignified, secretive, honorable people – will often choose somebody like Brian, will waste their helpless love on some vicious, silly person who is not even evil, or a monster, but just some importunate nuisance? I decided that Herb, with all his gentleness and carefulness, was avenging himself on us all – not just on Gladys but on us all – with Brian, and that what he was feeling when I studied his face must have been a savage and gleeful scorn. But embarrassment as well – embarrassment for Brian and for himself and for Gladys, and to some degree for all of us. Shame for all of us – that is what I thought then.

Later still, I backed off from this explanation. I got to a stage of backing off from the things I couldn't really know. It's enough for me now just to think of Herb's face with that peculiar, stricken look; to think of Brian monkeying in the shade of Herb's dignity; to think of my own mystified concentration on Herb, my need to catch him out, if I could ever get the chance, and then move in and stay close to him. How attractive, how delectable, the prospect of intimacy is, with the very person who will never grant it. I can still feel the pull of a man like that, of his promising and refusing.

I would still like to know things. Never mind facts. Never mind theories, either.

When I finished my drink I wanted to say something to Herb. I stood beside him and waited for a moment when he was not listening to or talking with anyone else and when the increasingly rowdy conversation of the others would cover what I had to say.

'I'm sorry your friend had to go away.'

'That's all right.'

Herb spoke kindly and with amusement, and so shut me off from any further right to look at or speak about his life. He knew what I was up to. He must have known it before, with lots of women. He knew how to deal with it.

Lily had a little more whisky in her mug and told how she and her best girlfriend (dead now, of liver trouble) had dressed up as men one time and gone into the men's side of the beer parlor, the side where it said MEN ONLY, because they wanted to see what it was like. They sat in a corner drinking beer and keeping their eyes and ears open, and nobody looked twice or thought a thing about them, but soon a problem arose.

'Where were we going to go? If we went around to the other side and anybody seen us going into the ladies', they would scream bloody murder. And if we went into the men's somebody'd be sure to notice we didn't do it the right way. Meanwhile the beer was going through us like a bugger!'

'What you don't do when you're young!' Marjorie said.

Several people gave me and Morgy advice. They told us to enjoy ourselves while we could. They told us to stay out of trouble. They said they had all been young once. Herb said we were a good crew and had done a good job but he didn't want to get in bad with any of the women's husbands by keeping them there too late. Marjorie and Lily expressed indifference to their husbands, but Irene announced that she loved hers and that it was not true that he had been dragged back from Detroit to marry her, no matter what people said. Henry said it was a good life if you didn't weaken. Morgan said he wished us all the most sincere Merry Christmas.

When we came out of the Turkey Barn it was snowing. Lily said it was like a Christmas card, and so it was, with the snow whirling around the streetlights in town and around the colored lights people had put up outside their doorways. Morgan was giving Henry and Irene a ride home in the truck, acknowledging age and pregnancy and Christmas. Morgy took a shortcut through the field, and Herb walked off by himself, head down and hands in his pockets, rolling slightly, as if he were on the deck of a lake boat. Marjorie and Lily linked arms with me as if we were old comrades.

'Let's sing,' Lily said. 'What'll we sing?'

'"We Three Kings"?' said Marjorie. '"We Three Turkey Gutters"?'

'"I'm Dreaming of a White Christmas."'

'Why dream? You got it!'

So we sang.

'Christmas at Thompson Hall'
by Anthony Trollope

Anthony Trollope was born on 24 April 1815. His family were poor and his mother supported them through writing. In 1834 Trollope began a life-long career in the General Post Office – he is credited with introducing the pillar box. He published his first novel in 1847, but his fourth novel, *The Warden* (1855), began the sequence of 'Barsetshire' novels for which he was to become best known. This series of five novels spanned twenty years of Trollope's career as a novelist, as did the 'Palliser' series. He wrote over 47 novels in total, as well as short stories, biographies, travel books and his own autobiography, which was published posthumously in 1883. Trollope died on 6 December 1882.

Read more by Anthony Trollope:
Can You Forgive Her?
The Warden
Barchester Towers

MRS BROWN'S SUCCESS

Everyone remembers the severity of the Christmas of 187-.
I will not designate the year more closely, lest I should enable
those who are too curious to investigate the circumstances
of this story, and inquire into details which I do not intend
to make known. That winter, however, was especially severe,
and the cold of the last ten days of December was more felt,
I think, in Paris than in any part of England. It may, indeed,
be doubted whether there is any town in any country in
which thoroughly bad weather is more afflicting than in the
French capital. Snow and hail seem to be colder there, and
fires certainly are less warm, than in London. And then
there is a feeling among visitors to Paris that Paris ought to
be gay; that gaiety, prettiness, and liveliness are its aims, as
money, commerce, and general business are the aims of
London, – which with its outside sombre darkness does
often seem to want an excuse for its ugliness. But on this
occasion, at this Christmas of 187-, Paris was neither gay nor
pretty nor lively. You could not walk the streets without
being ankle deep, not in snow, but in snow that had just

become slush; and there were falling throughout the day and night of the 23rd of December a succession of damp half-frozen abominations from the sky which made it almost impossible for men and women to go about their business.

It was at ten o'clock on that evening that an English lady and gentleman arrived at the Grand Hotel on the Boulevard des Italiens. As I have reasons for concealing the names of this married couple I will call them Mr and Mrs Brown. Now I wish it to be understood that in all the general affairs of life this gentleman and this lady lived happily together, with all the amenities which should bind a husband and a wife. Mrs Brown was one of a wealthy family, and Mr Brown, when he married her, had been relieved from the necessity of earning his bread. Nevertheless she had at once yielded to him when he expressed a desire to spend the winters of their life in the South of France; and he, though he was by disposition somewhat idle, and but little prone to the energetic occupations of life, would generally allow himself, at other periods of the year, to be carried hither and thither by her, whose more robust nature delighted in the excitement of travelling. But on this occasion there had been a little difference between them.

Early in December an intimation had reached Mrs Brown at Pau that on the coming Christmas there was to be a great gathering of all the Thompsons in the Thompson family hall at Stratford-le-Bow, and that she who had been a Thompson was desired to join the party with her husband. On this occasion her only sister was desirous of introducing to the family generally a most excellent young man to whom she had recently become engaged. The Thompsons, – the real name, however, is in fact concealed, – were a numerous and a thriving people. There were uncles and cousins and brothers who had all done well in the world, and who were all likely to do better still. One had lately been returned to Parliament for the Essex Flats, and was at the time of which I am writing a conspicuous member of the gallant Conservative majority. It was partly in triumph at this success that the great Christmas gathering of the Thompsons was to be held, and an opinion had been expressed by the legislator himself that should Mrs Brown, with her husband, fail to join the family on this happy occasion she and he would be regarded as being *fainéant* Thompsons.

Since her marriage, which was an affair now nearly eight years old, Mrs Brown had never passed a Christmas in England. The desirability of doing so had often been mooted by her. Her very soul craved the festivities of holly and mincepies. There had ever been meetings of the Thompsons at Thompson Hall, though meetings not so significant, not so important to the family, as this one which was now to be collected. More than once had she expressed a wish to see old Christmas again in the old house among the old faces. But her husband had always pleaded a certain weakness about his throat and chest as a reason for remaining among the delights of Pau. Year after year she had yielded; and now this loud summons had come.

It was not without considerable trouble that she had induced Mr Brown to come as far as Paris. Most unwillingly had he left Pau; and then, twice on his journey, – both at Bordeaux and Tours, – he had made an attempt to return. From the first moment he had pleaded his throat, and when at last he had consented to make the journey he had stipulated for sleeping at those two towns and at Paris. Mrs Brown, who, without the slightest feeling of fatigue, could have made the journey from Pau to Stratford without stopping, had assented to everything, – so that they might be at Thompson Hall on Christmas Eve. When Mr Brown uttered his unavailing complaints at the two first towns at which they stayed, she did not perhaps quite believe all that he said of his own condition. We know how prone the strong are to suspect the weakness of the weak, – as the weak are to be disgusted by the strength of the strong. There were perhaps a few words between them on the journey, but the result had hitherto been in favour of the lady. She had succeeded in bringing Mr Brown as far as Paris.

Had the occasion been less important, no doubt she would have yielded. The weather had been bad even when they left Pau, but as they had made their way northwards it had become worse and still worse. As they left Tours Mr Brown, in a hoarse whisper, had declared his conviction that the journey would kill him. Mrs Brown, however, had unfortunately noticed half an hour before that he had scolded the waiter on the score of an over-charged franc or two with a loud and clear voice. Had she really believed that there was danger, or even suffering, she would have yielded; – but no woman is satisfied in such a matter to be taken in by false pretences. She observed that he ate a good dinner on his way to Paris, and that he took a small glass of cognac with complete relish, – which a man really suffering from bronchitis surely would not do. So she persevered, and brought him into Paris, late in the evening, in the midst of all that slush and snow. Then, as they sat down to supper, she thought that he did speak hoarsely, and her loving feminine heart began to misgive her.

But this now was at any rate clear to her, – that he could not be worse off by going on to London than he would be should he remain in Paris. If a man is to be ill he had better be ill in the bosom of his family than at a hotel. What comfort could he have, what relief, in that huge barrack? As for the cruelty of the weather, London could not be worse than Paris, and then she thought she had heard that sea air is good for a sore throat. In that bedroom which had been allotted to them *au quatrième*, they could not even get a decent fire. It would in every way be wrong now to forego the great Christmas gathering when nothing could be gained by staying in Paris.

She had perceived that as her husband became really ill he became also more tractable and less disputatious.

Immediately after that little glass of cognac he had declared that he would be — if he would go beyond Paris, and she began to fear that, after all, everything would have been done in vain. But as they went down to supper between ten and eleven he was more subdued, and merely remarked that this journey would, he was sure, be the death of him. It was half-past eleven when they got back to their bedroom, and then he seemed to speak with good sense, – and also with much real apprehension. 'If I can't get something to relieve me I know I shall never make my way on,' he said. It was intended that they should leave the hotel at half-past five the next morning, so as to arrive at Stratford, travelling by the tidal train, at half-past seven on Christmas Eve. The early hour, the long journey, the infamous weather, the prospect of that horrid gulf between Boulogne and Folkestone, would have been as nothing to Mrs Brown, had it not been for that settled look of anguish which had now pervaded her husband's face. 'If you don't find something to relieve me I shall never live through it,' he said again, sinking back into the questionable comfort of a Parisian hotel arm-chair.

'But, my dear, what can I do?' she asked, almost in tears, standing over him and caressing him. He was a thin, genteel-looking man, with a fine long, soft brown beard, a little bald at the top of the head, but certainly a genteel-looking man. She loved him dearly, and in her softer moods was apt to spoil him with her caresses. 'What can

I do, my dearie? You know I would do anything if I could. Get into bed, my pet, and be warm, and then tomorrow morning you will be all right.' At this moment he was preparing himself for his bed, and she was assisting him. Then she tied a piece of flannel round his throat, and kissed him, and put him in beneath the bedclothes.

'I'll tell you what you can do,' he said very hoarsely. His voice was so bad now that she could hardly hear him. So she crept close to him, and bent over him. She would do anything if he would only say what. Then he told her what was his plan. Down in the salon he had seen a large jar of mustard standing on a sideboard. As he left the room he had observed that this had not been withdrawn with the other appurtenances of the meal. If she could manage to find her way down there, taking with her a handkerchief folded for the purpose, and if she could then appropriate a part of the contents of that jar, and returning with her prize, apply it to his throat, he thought that he could get some relief, so that he might be able to leave his bed the next morning at five. 'But I am afraid it will be very disagreeable for you to go down all alone at this time of night,' he croaked out in a piteous whisper.

'Of course I'll go,' said she. 'I don't mind going in the least. Nobody will bite me,' and she at once began to fold a clean handkerchief. 'I won't be two minutes, my darling, and if there is a grain of mustard in the house I'll have it on your chest almost immediately.' She was a woman not easily cowed, and the journey down into the salon was nothing to her. Before she went she tucked the clothes carefully up to his ears, and then she started.

To run along the first corridor till she came to a flight of stairs was easy enough, and easy enough to descend them. Then there was another corridor, and another flight, and a third corridor and a third flight, and she began to think that she was wrong. She found herself in a part of the hotel which she had not hitherto visited, and soon discovered by looking through an open door or two that she had found her way among a set of private sitting-rooms which she had not seen before. Then she tried to make her way back, up the same stairs and through the same passages, so that she might start again. She was beginning to think that she had lost herself altogether, and that she would be able to find neither the salon nor her bedroom, when she happily met the night-porter. She was dressed in a loose white dressing-gown, with a white net over her loose hair, and with white worsted slippers. I ought perhaps to have described her personal appearance sooner. She was a large woman, with a commanding bust, thought by some to be handsome, after the manner of Juno. But with strangers there was a certain severity of manner about her, – a fortification, as it were, of her virtue against all possible attacks, – a declared determination to maintain at all points, the beautiful character of a British matron, which, much as it had been appreciated at Thompson Hall, had met with some ill-natured criticism among French men and women. At Pau she had been called La

Fière Anglaise. The name had reached her own ears and those of her husband. He had been much annoyed, but she had taken it in good part, – and had endeavoured to live up to it. With her husband she could, on occasion, be soft, but she was of the opinion that with other men a British matron should be stern. She was now greatly in want of assistance; but, nevertheless, when she met the porter she remembered her character. 'I have lost my way wandering through these horrid passages,' she said, in her severest tone. This was in answer to some question from him, – some question to which her reply was given very slowly. Then when he asked where Madame wished to go, she paused, again thinking what destination she would announce. No doubt the man could take her back to her bedroom, but if so, the mustard must be renounced, and with the mustard, as she now feared, all hope of reaching Thompson Hall on Christmas Eve. But she, though she was in many respects a brave woman, did not dare to tell the man that she was prowling about the hotel in order that she might make a midnight raid upon the mustard pot. She paused, therefore, for a moment, that she might collect her thoughts, erecting her head as she did so in her best Juno fashion, till the porter was lost in admiration. Thus she gained time to fabricate a tale. She had, she said, dropped her handkerchief under the supper table; would he show her the way to the salon, in order that she might pick it up. But the porter did more than that, and accompanied her to the room in which she had supped.

Here, of course, there was a prolonged, and, it need hardly be said, a vain search. The good-natured man insisted on emptying an enormous receptacle of soiled table-napkins, and on turning them over one by one, in order that the lady's property might be found. The lady stood by unhappy, but still patient, and, as the man was stooping to his work, her eye was on the mustard pot. There it was, capable of containing enough to blister the throats of a score of sufferers. She edged off a little towards it while the man was busy, trying to persuade herself that he would surely forgive her if she took the mustard, and told him her whole story. But the descent from her Juno bearing would have been so great! She must have owned, not only to the quest for mustard, but also to a fib, – and she could not do it. The porter was at last of the opinion that Madame must have made a mistake, and Madame acknowledged that she was afraid it was so.

With a longing, lingering eye, with an eye turned back, oh! so sadly, to the great jar, she left the room, the porter leading the way. She assured him that she would find it by herself, but he would not leave her till he had put her on to the proper passage. The journey seemed to be longer now even than before, but as she ascended the many stairs she swore to herself that she would not even yet be baulked of her object. Should her husband want comfort for his poor throat, and the comfort be there within her reach, and he not have it? She counted every stair as she went up, and marked every turn well. She was sure now that she would know the way, and that she could return to the room without fault. She would go back to the salon. Even though the man should encounter her again, she would go boldly forward and seize the remedy which her poor husband so grievously required.

'Ah, yes,' she said, when the porter told her that her room, No. 333, was in the corridor which they had then reached, 'I know it all now. I am so much obliged. Do not come a step further.' He was anxious to accompany her up to the very door, but she stood in the passage and prevailed. He lingered awhile – naturally. Unluckily she had brought no money with her, and could not give him the two-franc piece which he had earned. Nor could she fetch it from her room, feeling that were she to return to her husband without the mustard no second attempt would be possible. The disappointed man turned on his heel at last, and made his way down the stairs and along the passage. It seemed to her to be almost an eternity while she listened to his still audible footsteps. She had gone on, creeping noiselessly up to the very door of her room, and there she stood, shading the candle in her hand, till she thought that the man must have wandered away into some furthest corner of that endless building. Then she turned once more and retraced her steps.

There was no difficulty now as to the way. She knew it, every stair. At the head of each flight she stood and listened, but not a sound was to be heard, and then she went on again. Her heart beat high with anxious desire to achieve her object, and at the same time with fear. What might have been explained so easily at first would now be as difficult of explanation. At last she was in the great public vestibule, which she was now visiting for the third time, and of which, at her last visit, she had taken the bearings accurately. The door was there – closed, indeed, but it opened easily to the hand. In the hall, and on the stairs, and along the passages, there had been gas, but here there was no light beyond that given by the little taper which she carried. When accompanied by the porter she had not feared the darkness, but now there was something in the obscurity which made her dread to walk the length of the room up to the mustard jar. She paused, and listened, and trembled. Then she thought of the glories of Thompson Hall, of the genial warmth of a British Christmas, of that proud legislator who was her first cousin, and with a rush she made good the distance, and laid her hand upon the copious delft. She looked round, but there was no one there; no sound was heard; not the distant creak of a shoe, not a rattle from one of those doors. As she paused with her fair hand upon the top of the jar, while the other held the white cloth on which the medicinal compound was to be placed, she looked like Lady Macbeth as she listened at Duncan's chamber door.

There was no doubt as to the sufficiency of the contents. The jar was full nearly up to the lips. The mixture was, no doubt, very different from that good wholesome English mustard which your cook makes fresh for you, with a little water, in two minutes. It was impregnated with a sour odour, and was, to English eyes, unwholesome of colour. But still it was mustard. She seized the horn spoon, and without further delay spread an ample sufficiency on the folded square of the handkerchief. Then she commenced to hurry her return.

But still there was a difficulty, no thought of which had occurred to her before. The candle occupied one hand, so that she had but the other for the sustenance of her treasure. Had she brought a plate or saucer from the salon, it would have been all well. As it was she was obliged to keep her eye intent on her right hand, and to proceed very slowly on her return journey. She was surprised to find what an aptitude the thing had to slip from her grasp. But still she progressed slowly, and was careful not to miss a turning. At last she was safe at her chamber door. There it was, No. 333.

MRS BROWN'S FAILURE

With her eye still fixed upon her burden, she glanced up at the number of the door – 333. She had been determined all through not to forget that. Then she turned the latch and crept in. The chamber also was dark after the gaslight on the stairs, but that was so much the better. She herself had put out the two candles on the dressing-table before she had left her husband. As she was closing the door behind her she paused, and could hear that he was sleeping. She was well aware that she had been long absent, – quite long enough for a man to fall into slumber who was given that way. She must have been gone, she thought, fully an hour. There had been no end to that turning over of napkins which she had so well known to be altogether vain. She paused at the centre table of the room, still looking at the mustard, which she now deli- cately dried from off her hand. She had had no idea that it would have been so difficult to carry so light and so small an affair. But there it was, and nothing had been lost. She took some small instrument from the washing-stand, and with the handle collected the flowing fragments into the centre. Then the question occurred to her whether, as her husband was sleeping so sweetly, it would be well to disturb him. She listened again, and felt that the slight murmur of a snore with which her ears were regaled was altogether free from any real malady in the throat. Then it occurred to her, that after all, fatigue perhaps had only made him cross. She bethought herself how, during the whole journey, she had failed to believe in his illness. What meals he had eaten! How thoroughly he had been able to enjoy his full complement of cigars! And then that glass of brandy, against which she had raised her voice slightly in feminine opposition. And now he was sleeping there like an infant, with full, round, perfected, almost sonorous workings of the throat. Who does not know that sound, almost of two rusty bits of iron scratching against each other, which comes from a suffering windpipe? There was no semblance of that here. Why disturb him when he was so thoroughly enjoying that rest which, more certainly than anything else, would fit him for the fatigue of the morrow's journey?

I think that, after all her labour, she would have left the pungent cataplasm on the table, and have crept gently into bed beside him, had not a thought suddenly struck her of the great injury he had been doing her if he were not really ill. To send her down there, in a strange hotel, wandering among the passages, in the middle of the night, subject to the contumely of any one who might meet her, on a commission which, if it were not sanctified by absolute necessity, would be so thoroughly objectionable! At this moment she hardly did believe that he had ever really been ill. Let him have the cataplasm; if not as a remedy, then as a punishment. It could, at any rate, do him no harm. It was with an idea of avenging rather than of justifying the past labours of the night that she proceeded at once to quick action.

Leaving the candle on the table so that she might steady her right hand with the left, she hurried stealthily to the bedside. Even though he was behaving badly to her, she would not cause him discomfort by waking him roughly. She would do a wife's duty to him as a British matron should. She would not only put the warm mixture on his neck, but would sit carefully by him for twenty minutes, so that she might relieve him from it when the proper

period should have come for removing the counter irritation from his throat. There would doubtless be some little
difficulty in this, – in collecting the mustard after it had
served her purpose. Had she been at home, surrounded by
her own comforts, the application would have been made
with some delicate linen bag, through which the pun-
gency of the spice would have penetrated with strength
sufficient for the purpose. But the circumstance of the
occasion had not admitted this. She had, she felt, done
wonders in achieving so much success as this which she
had obtained. If there should be anything disagreeable in
the operation he must submit to it. He had asked for mustard for his throat, and mustard he should have.

As these thoughts passed quickly through her mind,
leaning over him in the dark, with her eye fixed on the
mixture lest it should slip, she gently raised his flowing
beard with her left hand, and with her other inverted rapidly, steadily but very softly fixed the handkerchief on his
throat. From the bottom of his chin to the spot at which
the collar bones meeting together form the orifice of the
chest it covered the whole noble expanse. There was
barely time for a glance, but never had she been more
conscious of the grand proportions of that manly throat.
A sweet feeling of pity came upon her, causing her to
determine to relieve his sufferings in the shorter space of
fifteen minutes. He had been lying on his back, with his
lips apart, and as she held back his beard, that and her
hand nearly covered the features of his face. But he made

no violent effort to free himself from the encounter. He did not even move an arm or a leg. He simply emitted a snore louder than any that had come before. She was aware that it was not his wont to be so loud – that there was generally something more delicate and perhaps more querulous in his nocturnal voice, but then the present circumstances were exceptional. She dropped the beard very softly – and there on the pillow before her lay the face of a stranger. She had put the mustard plaster on the wrong man.

Not Priam wakened in the dead of night, not Dido when first she learned that Aeneas had fled, not Othello when he learned that Desdemona had been chaste, not Medea when she became conscious of her slaughtered children, could have been more struck with horror than was this British matron as she stood for a moment gazing with awe on that stranger's bed. One vain, half-completed, snatching grasp she made at the handkerchief, and then drew back her hand. If she were to touch him would he not wake at once, and find her standing there in his bedroom? And then how could she explain it? By what words could she so quickly make him know the circumstances of that strange occurrence that he should accept it all before he had said a word that might offend her? For a moment she stood all but paralysed after that faint ineffectual movement of her arm. Then he stirred his head uneasily on the pillow, opened wider his lips, and twice in rapid succession snored louder than before. She started back a couple of paces, and with her body placed between him and the candle, with her face averted, but with her hand still resting on the foot of the bed, she endeavoured to think what duty required of her.

She had injured the man. Though she had done it most unwittingly, there could be no doubt but that she had injured him. If for a moment she could be brave, the injury might in truth be little; but how disastrous might be the consequences if she were now in her cowardice to leave him, who could tell? Applied for fifteen or twenty minutes a mustard plaster may be the salvation of a throat ill at ease, but if left there throughout the night upon the neck of a strong man, ailing nothing, only too prone in his strength to slumber soundly, how sad, how painful, for aught she knew how dangerous might be the effects! And surely it was an error which any man with a heart in his bosom would pardon! Judging from what little she had seen of him she thought that he must have a heart in his bosom. Was it not her duty to wake him, and then quietly to extricate him from the embarrassment which she had brought upon him?

But in doing this what words should she use? How should she wake him? How should she make him understand her goodness, her beneficence, her sense of duty, before he should have jumped from the bed and rushed to the bell, and have summoned all above and all below to the rescue? 'Sir, do not move, do not stir, do not scream. I have put a mustard plaster on your throat, thinking that you were my husband. As yet no harm has been done. Let me take it off, and then hold your peace forever.' Where is the man of such native constancy and grace of spirit that, at the first moment of waking with a shock, he could hear these words from the mouth of an unknown woman by his bedside, and at once obey them to the letter? Would he not surely jump from his bed, with that horrid compound falling about him, – from which there could be no complete relief unless he would keep his present attitude without a motion. The picture which presented itself to her mind as to his probable conduct was so terrible that she found herself unable to incur the risk.

Then an idea presented itself to her mind. We all know how in a moment quick thoughts will course through the subtle brain. She would find that porter and send him to explain it all. There should be no concealment now. She would tell the story and would bid him to find the necessary aid. Alas! as she told herself that she would do so, she knew well that she was only running from the danger which it was her duty to encounter. Once again she put out her hand as though to return along the bed. Then thrice he snorted louder than before, and moved up his knee uneasily beneath the clothes as though the sharpness of the mustard were already working upon his skin. She watched him for a moment longer, and then, with the candle in her hand, she fled.

Poor human nature! Had he been an old man, even a middle-aged man, she would not have left him to his

unmerited sufferings. As it was, though she completely
recognised her duty, and knew what justice and goodness
demanded of her, she could not do it. But there was still
left to her that plan of sending the night-porter to him. It
was not till she was out of the room and had gently closed
the door behind her, that she began to bethink herself
how she had made the mistake. With a glance of her eye
she looked up, and then saw the number on the door: 353.
Remarking to herself, with a Briton's natural criticism on
things French, that those horrid foreigners do not know
how to make their figures, she scudded rather than ran
along the corridor, and then down some stairs and along
another passage, – so that she might not be found in the
neighbourhood should the poor man in his agony rush
rapidly from his bed.

In the confusion of her first escape she hardly ventured
to look for her own passage, – nor did she in the least know
how she had lost her way when she came upstairs with the
mustard in her hand. But at the present moment her chief
object was the night-porter. She went on descending till
she came again to that vestibule, and looking up at the
clock saw that it was now past one. It was not yet midnight
when she left her husband, but she was not at all astonished at the lapse of time. It seemed to her as though she
had passed a night among these miseries. And, oh, what a
night! But there was yet much to be done. She must find
that porter, and then return to her own suffering husband.
Ah, – what now should she say to him! If he should really

be ill, how should she assuage him? And yet how more than ever necessary was it that they should leave that hotel early in the morning, – that they should leave Paris by the very earliest and quickest train that would take them as fugitives from their present dangers! The door of the salon was open, but she had no courage to go in search of a second supply. She would have lacked strength to carry it up the stairs. Where now, oh, where, was that man? From the vestibule she made her way into the hall, but everything seemed to be deserted. Through the glass she could see a light in the court beyond, but she could not bring herself to endeavour even to open the hall doors.

And now she was very cold, – chilled to her very bones. All this had been done at Christmas, and during such severity of weather as had never before been experienced by living Parisians. A feeling of great pity for herself gradually came upon her. What wrong had she done that she should be so grievously punished? Why should she be driven to wander about in this way till her limbs were failing her? And then, so absolutely important as it was that her strength should support her in the morning! The man would not die even though he were left there without aid, to rid himself of the cataplasm as best he might. Was it absolutely necessary that she should disgrace herself?

But she could not even procure the means of disgracing herself, if that telling her story to the night-porter would have been, a disgrace. She did not find him, and at last resolved to make her way back to her own room without further quest. She began to think that she had done all that she could do. No man was ever killed by a mustard plaster on his throat. His discomfort at the worst would not be worse than hers had been – or too probably than that of her poor husband. So she went back up the stairs and along the passages, and made her way on this occasion to the door of her room without any difficulty. The way was so well known to her that she could not but wonder that she had failed before. But now her hands had been empty, and her eyes had been at her full command. She looked up, and there was the number, very manifest on this occasion, – 333. She opened the door most gently, thinking that her husband might be sleeping as soundly as that other man had slept, and she crept into the room.

MRS BROWN ATTEMPTS TO ESCAPE

But her husband was not sleeping. He was not even in bed, as she had left him. She found him sitting there before the fireplace, on which one half-burned log still retained a spark of what had once pretended to be a fire. Nothing more wretched than his appearance could be imagined. There was a single lighted candle on the table, on which he was leaning with his two elbows, while his head rested between his hands. He had on a dressing-gown over his night-shirt, but otherwise was not clothed. He shivered audibly, or rather shook himself with the cold, and made the table to chatter as she entered the room. Then he groaned, and let his head fall from his hands on to the table. It occurred to her at the moment as she recognised the tone of his querulous voice, and as she saw the form of his neck, that she must have been deaf and blind when she had mistaken that stalwart stranger for her husband. 'Oh, my dear,' she said, 'why are you not in bed?' He answered nothing in words, but only groaned again. 'Why did you get up? I left you warm and comfortable.'

'Where have you been all night?' he half whispered, half croaked, with an agonising effort.

'I have been looking for the mustard.'

'Have been looking all night and haven't found it? Where have you been?'

She refused to speak a word to him till she had got him into bed, and then she told her story. But, alas, that which she told was not the true story! As she was persuading him to go back to his rest, and while she arranged the clothes again around him, she with difficulty made up her mind as to what she would do and what she would say. Living or dying he must be made to start for Thompson Hall at half-past five on the next morning. It was no longer a question of the amenities of Christmas, no longer a mere desire to satisfy the family ambition of her own people, no longer an anxiety to see her new brother-in-law. She was conscious that there was in that house one whom she had deeply injured, and from whose vengeance, even from whose aspect, she must fly. How could she endure to see that face which she was so well sure that she would recognise, or to hear the slightest sound of that voice which would be quite familiar to her ears, though it had never spoken a word in her hearing? She must certainly fly on the wings of the earliest train which would carry her towards the old house; but in order that she might do so she must propitiate her husband.

So she told her story. She had gone forth, as he had bade her, in search of the mustard, and then had suddenly lost her way. Up and down the house she had wandered, perhaps nearly a dozen times. 'Had she met no one?' he asked in that raspy, husky whisper. 'Surely there must have been some one about the hotel! Nor was it possible that she could have been roaming about all those hours.' 'Only one hour, my dear,' she said. Then there was a question about the duration of time, in which both of them waxed angry, and as she became angry her husband waxed stronger, and as he became violent beneath the clothes the comfortable idea returned to her that he was not perhaps so ill as he would seem to be. She found herself driven to tell him something about the porter, having to account for that lapse of time by explaining how she had driven the poor man to search for the handkerchief which she had never lost.

'Why did you not tell him you wanted the mustard?'

'My dear!'

'Why not? There is nothing to be ashamed of in wanting mustard.'

'At one o'clock in the morning! I couldn't do it. To tell you the truth, he wasn't very civil, and I thought that he was, – perhaps a little tipsy. Now, my dear, do go to sleep.'

'Why didn't you get the mustard?'

'There was none there, – nowhere at all about the room. I went down again and searched everywhere. That's what took me so long. They always lock up those kind of things at these French hotels. They are too close-fisted to leave anything out. When you first spoke of it I knew that it would be gone when I got there. Now, my dear, do go to sleep, because we positively must start in the morning.'

'That is impossible,' said he, jumping up in the bed.

'We must go, my dear. I say that we must go. After all that has passed I wouldn't not be with Uncle John and my cousin Robert tomorrow evening for more, – more, – more than I would venture to say.'

'Bother!' he exclaimed.

'It's all very well for you to say that, Charles, but you don't know. I say that we must go tomorrow, and we will.'

'I do believe you want to kill me, Mary.'

'That is very cruel, Charles, and most false, and most unjust. As for making you ill, nothing could be so bad for you as this wretched place, where nobody can get warm either day or night. If anything will cure your throat for you at once it will be the sea air. And only think how much more comfortable they can make you at Thompson Hall than anywhere in this country. I have so set my heart upon it, Charles, that I will do it. If we are not there tomorrow night Uncle John won't consider us as belonging to the family.'

'I don't believe a word of it.'

'Jane told me so in her letter. I wouldn't let you know before because I thought it so unjust. But that has been the reason why I've been so earnest about it all through.'

It was a thousand pities that so good a woman should have been driven by the sad stress of circumstances to tell so many fibs. One after another she was compelled to invent them, that there might be a way open to her of escaping the horrors of a prolonged sojourn in that hotel. At length, after much grumbling, he became silent, and she trusted that he was sleeping. He had not as yet said that he would start at the required hour in the morning, but she was perfectly determined in her own mind that he should be made to do so. As he lay there motionless, and as she wandered about the room pretending to pack her things, she more than once almost resolved that she would tell him everything. Surely then he would be ready to make any effort. But there came upon her an idea that he might perhaps fail to see all the circumstances, and that, so failing, he would insist on remaining that he might tender some apology to the injured gentleman. An apology might have been very well had she not left him there in his misery – but what apology would be possible now? She would have to see him and speak to him, and everyone in the hotel would know every detail of the story. Everyone in France would know that it was she who had gone to the strange man's bedside, and put the mustard plaster on the strange man's throat in the dead of night! She could not tell the story even to her husband, lest even her husband should betray her.

Her own sufferings at the present moment were not light. In her perturbation of mind she had foolishly resolved that she would not herself go to bed. The tragedy of the night had seemed to her too deep for personal comfort. And then how would it be were she to sleep, and have no one to call her? It was imperative that she should have all her powers ready for thoroughly arousing him. It occurred to her that the servant of the hotel would certainly run her too short of time. She had to work for herself and for him too, and therefore she would not sleep. But she was very cold, and she put on first a shawl over her dressing-gown and then a cloak. She could not consume all the remaining hours of the night in packing one bag and one portmanteau, so that at last she sat down on the narrow red cotton velvet sofa, and, looking at her watch, perceived that as yet it was not much past two o'clock. How was she to get through those other three long, tedious, chilly hours?

Then there came a voice from the bed — 'Ain't you coming?'

'I hoped you were asleep, my dear.'

'I haven't been asleep at all. You'd better come, if you don't mean to make yourself as ill as I am.'

'You are not so very bad, are you, darling?'

'I don't know what you call bad. I never felt my throat so choked in my life before!' Still as she listened she thought that she remembered his throat to have been more choked. If the husband of her bosom could play with her feelings and deceive her on such an occasion as this, – then, then, – then she thought that she would rather not have any husband of her bosom at all. But she did creep into bed, and lay down beside him without saying another word.

Of course she slept, but her sleep was not the sleep of the blest. At every striking of the clock in the quadrangle she would start up in alarm, fearing that she had let the time go by. Though the night was so short it was very long to her. But he slept like an infant. She could hear from his breathing that he was not quite so well as she could wish him to be, but still he was resting in beautiful tranquility. Not once did he move when she started up, as she did so frequently. Orders had been given and repeated over and over again that they should be called at five. The man in the office had almost been angry as he assured Mrs Brown for the fourth time that Monsieur and Madame would most assuredly be wakened at the appointed time. But still she would trust no one, and was up and about the room before the clock had struck half-past four.

In her heart of hearts she was very tender towards her husband. Now, in order that he might feel a gleam of warmth while he was dressing himself, she collected together the fragments of half-burned wood, and endeavoured to make a little fire. Then she took out from her bag a small pot, and a patent lamp, and some chocolate, and prepared for him a warm drink, so that he might have it instantly as he was awakened. She would do anything for him in the way of ministering to his comfort – only he must go! Yes, he certainly must go!

And then she wondered how that strange man was bearing himself at the present moment. She would fain have ministered to him too had it been possible; but ah! – it was so impossible! Probably before this he would have been aroused from his troubled slumbers. But then – how aroused? At what time in the night would the burning heat upon his chest have awakened him to a sense of torture which must have been so altogether incomprehensible to him? Her strong imagination showed to her a clear picture of the scene, – clear, though it must have been done in the dark. How he must have tossed and hurled himself under the clothes; how those strong knees must have worked themselves up and down before the potent god of sleep would allow him to return to perfect consciousness; how his fingers, restrained by no reason, would have trampled over his feverish throat, scattering everywhere that unhappy poultice! Then when he should have sat up wide awake, but still in the dark – with her mind's eye she saw it all – feeling that some fire as from the infernal regions had fallen upon him but whence he would know not, how fiercely wild would be the working of his spirit! Ah, now she knew, now she felt, now she acknowledged how bound she had been to awaken him at the moment, whatever might have been the personal inconvenience to herself! In such a position what would he do – or rather what had he done? She could follow much of it in her own thoughts; – how he would scramble madly from his bed, and with one hand still on his throat, would snatch hurriedly at the matches with the other. How the light would come, and how then he would rush to the mirror. Ah, what a sight he would behold! She could see it all to the last widespread daub.

But she could not see, she could not tell herself, what in such a position a man would do; – at any rate, not what that man would do. Her husband, she thought, would tell his wife, and then the two of them, between them, would – put up with it. There are misfortunes which, if they be published, are simply aggravated by ridicule. But she remembered the features of the stranger as she had seen them at that instant in which she had dropped his beard, and she thought that there was a ferocity in them, a certain tenacity of self-importance, which would not permit their owner to endure such treatment in silence. Would he not storm and rage, and ring the bell, and call all Paris to witness his revenge?

But the storming and the raging had not reached her yet, and now it wanted but a quarter to five. In three-quarters of an hour they would be in that demi-omnibus which they had ordered for themselves, and in half-an-hour after that they would be flying towards Thompson Hall. Then she allowed herself to think of those coming comforts, – of those comforts so sweet, if only they would come! That very day now present to her was the 24th of December, and on that very evening she would be sitting in Christmas joy among all her uncles and cousins, holding her new brother-in-law affectionately by the hand. Oh, what a change from Pandemonium to Paradise; – from that wretched room, from that miserable house in which there was such ample cause for fear, to all the domestic Christmas bliss of the home of the Thompsons! She resolved that she would not, at any rate, be deterred by any light opposition on the part of her husband. 'It wants just a quarter to five,' she said, putting her hand steadily upon his shoulder, 'and I'll get a cup of chocolate for you, so that you may get up comfortably.'

'I've been thinking about it,' he said, rubbing his eyes with the back of his hands. 'It will be so much better to go over by the mail train tonight. We should be in time for Christmas just the same.'

'That will not do at all,' she answered, energetically. 'Come, Charles, after all the trouble do not disappoint me.'

'It is such a horrid grind.'

'Think what I have gone through, – what I have done for you! In twelve hours we shall be there, among them all. You won't be so little like a man as not to go on now.' He threw himself back upon the bed, and tried to readjust the clothes round his neck. 'No, Charles, no,' she continued; 'not if I know it. Take your chocolate and get up. There is not a moment to be lost.' With that she laid her hand upon his shoulder, and made him clearly understand that he would not be allowed to take further rest in that bed.

Grumbling, sulky, coughing continually, and declaring that life under such circumstances was not worth having, he did at last get up and dress himself. When once she saw that he was obeying her she became again tender to him, and certainly took much more than her own share of the trouble of the proceedings. Long before the time was up she was ready, and the porter had been summoned to take the luggage downstairs. When the man came she was rejoiced to see that it was not he whom she had met among the passages during her nocturnal rambles. He shouldered the box, and told them that they would find coffee and bread and butter in the small *salle-à-manger* below.

'I told you that it would be so, when you would boil that stuff,' said the ungrateful man, who had nevertheless swallowed the hot chocolate when it was given to him.

They followed their luggage down into the hall; but as she went, at every step, the lady looked around her. She dreaded the sight of that porter of the night; she feared lest some potential authority of the hotel should come to her and ask her some horrid question; but of all her fears her greatest fear was that there should arise before her an apparition of that face which she had seen recumbent on its pillow.

As they passed the door of the great salon, Mr. Brown looked in. 'Why, there it is still!' said he.

'What?' said she, trembling in every limb.

'The mustard pot!'

'They have put it in there since,' she exclaimed energetically, in her despair. 'But never mind. The omnibus is here. Come away.' And she absolutely took him by the arm.

But at that moment a door behind them opened, and Mrs Brown heard herself called by her name. And there was the night-porter, – with a handkerchief in his hand. But the further doings of that morning must be told in a further chapter.

MRS BROWN DOES ESCAPE

It had been visible to Mrs Brown from the first moment of her arrival on the ground floor that 'something was the matter,' if we may be allowed to use such a phrase; and she felt all but convinced that this something had reference to her. She fancied that the people of the hotel were looking at her as she swallowed, or tried to swallow, her coffee. When her husband was paying the bill there was something disagreeable in the eye of the man who was taking the money. Her sufferings were very great, and no one sympathised with her. Her husband was quite at his ease, except that he was complaining of the cold. When she was anxious to get him out into the carriage, he still stood there leisurely, arranging shawl after shawl around his throat. 'You can do that quite as well in the omnibus,' she had just said to him very crossly, when there appeared upon the scene through a side door that very porter whom she dreaded, with a soiled pocket- handkerchief in his hand.

Even before the sound of her own name met her ears Mrs Brown knew it all. She understood the full horror of her position from that man's hostile face, and from the little article which he held in his hand. If during the watches of the night she had had money in her pocket, if she had made a friend of this greedy fellow by well-timed liberality, all might have been so different! But she reflected that she had allowed him to go unfee'd after all his trouble, and she knew that he was her enemy. It was the handkerchief that she feared. She thought that she might have brazened out anything but that. No one had seen her enter or leave that strange man's room. No one had seen her dip her hands in that jar. She had, no doubt, been found wandering about the house while the slumberer had been made to suffer so strangely, and there might have been suspicion, and perhaps accusation. But she would have been ready with frequent protestations to deny all charges made against her, and, though no one might have believed her, no one could have convicted her. Here, however, was evidence against which she would be unable to stand for a moment. At the first glance she acknowledged the potency of that damning morsel of linen.

During all the horrors of the night she had never given a thought to the handkerchief, and yet she ought to have known that the evidence it would bring against her was palpable and certain. Her name, 'M. Brown,' was plainly written on the corner. What a fool she had been not to have thought of this! Had she but remembered the plain marking which she, as a careful, well-conducted, British matron, had put upon all her clothes, she would at any hazard have recovered the article. Oh that she had waked the man, or bribed the porter, or even told her husband! But now she was, as it were, friendless, without support, without a word that she could say in her own defence, convicted of having committed this assault upon a strange man as he slept in his own bedroom, and then of having left him! The thing must be explained by the truth; but how to explain such truth, how to tell such story in a way to satisfy injured folk, and she with barely time sufficient to catch the train! Then it occurred to her that they could have no legal right to stop her because the pocket-handkerchief had been found in a strange gentleman's bedroom. 'Yes, it is mine,' she said, turning to her husband, as the porter, with a loud voice, asked if she were not Madame Brown. 'Take it, Charles, and come on.' Mr. Brown naturally stood still in astonishment. He did put out his hand, but the porter would not allow the evidence to pass so readily out of his custody.

'What does it all mean?' asked Mr. Brown.

'A gentleman has been – eh – eh –. Something has been done to a gentleman in his bedroom,' said the clerk.

'Something done to a gentleman!' repeated Mr Brown.

'Something very bad indeed,' said the porter. 'Look here,' and he showed the condition of the handkerchief.

'Charles, we shall lose the train,' said the affrighted wife.

'What the mischief does it all mean?' demanded the husband.

'Did Madame go into the gentleman's room?' asked the clerk. Then there was an awful silence, and all eyes were fixed upon the lady.

'What does it all mean?' demanded the husband. 'Did you go into anybody's room?'

'I did,' said Mrs. Brown with much dignity, looking round upon her enemies as a stag at bay will look upon the hounds which are attacking him. 'Give me the handkerchief.' But the night-porter quickly put it behind his back. 'Charles, we cannot allow ourselves to be delayed. You shall write a letter to the keeper of the hotel, explaining it all.' Then she essayed to swim out, through the front door, into the courtyard in which the vehicle was waiting for them. But three or four men and women interposed themselves, and even her husband did not seem quite ready to continue his journey. 'Tonight is Christmas Eve,' said Mrs Brown, 'and we shall not be at Thompson Hall! Think of my sister!'

'Why did you go into the man's bedroom, my dear?' whispered Mr Brown in English.

But the porter heard the whisper, and understood the language; — the porter who had not been 'tipped.' 'Ye'es; – vy?' asked the porter.

'It was a mistake, Charles; there is not a moment to lose. I can explain it all to you in the carriage.' Then the clerk suggested that Madame had better postpone her journey a little. The gentleman upstairs had certainly been very badly treated, and had demanded to know why so great an outrage had been perpetrated. The clerk said that he did not wish to send for the police – here Mrs Brown gasped terribly and threw herself on her husband's shoulder, – but he did not think he could allow the party to go till the gentleman upstairs had received some satisfaction. It had now become clearly impossible that the journey could be made by the early train. Even Mrs Brown gave it up herself, and demanded of her husband that she should be taken back to her bedroom.

'But what is to be said to the gentleman?' asked the porter.

Of course it was impossible that Mrs Brown should be made to tell her story there in the presence of them all. The clerk, when he found he had succeeded in preventing her from leaving the house, was satisfied with a promise from Mr Brown that he would inquire from his wife what were these mysterious circumstances, and would then come down to the office and give some explanation. If it were necessary, he would see the strange gentleman, – whom he now ascertained to be a certain Mr Jones returning from the east of Europe. He learned also that this Mr Jones had been most anxious to travel by that very morning train which he and his wife had intended to use, – that Mr Jones had been most particular in giving his orders accordingly, but that at the last moment he had declared himself to be unable even to dress himself, because of the injury which had been done him during the night. When Mr Brown heard this from the clerk just before he was allowed to take his wife upstairs, while she was sitting on a sofa in a corner with her face hidden, a look of awful gloom came over his own countenance. What could it be that his wife had done to the gentleman of so terrible a nature? 'You had better come up with me,' he said to her with marital severity, and the poor cowed woman went with him tamely as might have done some patient Grizel. Not a word was spoken till they were in the room and the door was locked. 'Now,' said he, 'what does it all mean?'

It was not till nearly two hours had passed that Mr Brown came down the stairs very slowly, – turning it all over in his mind. He had now gradually heard the absolute and exact truth, and had very gradually learned to believe it. It was first necessary that he should understand that his wife had told him many fibs during the night; but, as she constantly alleged to him when he complained of her conduct in this respect, they had all been told on his behalf. Had she not struggled to get the mustard for his comfort, and when she had secured the prize had she not hurried to put it on, – as she had fondly thought, – his throat? And though she had fibbed to him afterwards, had she not done so in order that he might not be troubled? 'You are not angry with me because I was in that man's room?' she asked, looking full into his eyes, but not quite without a sob. He paused a moment, and then declared, with something of a true husband's confidence in his tone, that he was not in the least angry with her on that account. Then she kissed him, and bade him remember that after all no one could really injure them. 'What harm has been done, Charles? The gentleman won't die because he has had a mustard plaster on his throat. The worst is about Uncle John and dear Jane. They do think so much of Christmas Eve at Thompson Hall!'

Mr Brown, when he again found himself in the clerk's office, requested that his card might be taken up to Mr Jones. Mr Jones had sent down his own card, which was handed to Mr Brown: 'Mr Barnaby Jones.' 'And how was it all, sir?' asked the clerk, in a whisper – a whisper which had at the same time something of authoritative demand and something also of submissive respect. The clerk of course was anxious to know the mystery. It is hardly too much to say that everyone in that vast hotel was by this time anxious to have the mystery unravelled. But Mr Brown would tell nothing to any one. 'It is merely a matter to be explained between me and Mr Jones,' he said. The card was taken upstairs, and after a while he was ushered into Mr Jones' room. It was, of course, that very 353 with which the reader is already acquainted. There was a fire burning, and the remains of Mr Jones' breakfast were on the table. He was sitting in his dressing-gown and slippers, with his shirt open in the front, and a silk handkerchief very loosely covering his throat. Mr Brown, as he entered the room, of course looked with considerable anxiety at the gentleman of whose condition he had heard so sad an account; but he could only observe some considerable stiffness of movement and demeanour as Mr Jones turned his head round to greet him.

'This has been a very disagreeable accident, Mr Jones,' said the husband of the lady.

'Accident! I don't know how it could have been an accident. It has been a most – most – most – a most monstrous, – er, – er, – I must say, interference with a gentleman's privacy, and personal comfort.'

'Quite so, Mr Jones, but, – on the part of the lady, who is my wife —'

'So I understand. I myself am about to become a married man, and I can understand what your feelings must be. I wish to say as little as possible to harrow them.' Here Mr. Brown bowed. 'But, – there's the fact. She did do it.'

'She thought it was – me!'

'What!'

'I give you my word as a gentleman, Mr Jones. When she was putting that mess upon you she thought it was me! She did, indeed.'

Mr Jones looked at his new acquaintance and shook his head. He did not think it possible that any woman would make such a mistake as that.

'I had a very bad sore throat,' continued Mr Brown, 'and indeed you may perceive it still,' – in saying this, he perhaps aggravated a little sign of his distemper, 'and I asked Mrs Brown to go down and get one, – just what she put on you.'

'I wish you'd had it,' said Mr Jones, putting his hand up to his neck.

'I wish I had, – for your sake as well as mine, – and for hers, poor woman. I don't know when she will get over the shock.'

'I don't know when I shall. And it has stopped me on my journey. I was to have been tonight, this very night, this Christmas Eve, with the young lady I am engaged to marry. Of course I couldn't travel. The extent of the injury done nobody can imagine at present.'

'It has been just as bad to me, sir. We were to have been with our family this Christmas Eve. There were particular reasons, — most particular. We were only hindered from going by hearing of your condition.'

'Why did she come into my room at all? I can't understand that. A lady always knows her own room at an hotel.'

'353 – that's yours; 333 – that's ours. Don't you see how easy it was? She had lost her way, and she was a little afraid lest the thing should fall down.'

'I wish it had, with all my heart.'

'That's how it was. Now I'm sure, Mr Jones, you'll take a lady's apology. It was a most unfortunate mistake, – most unfortunate; but what more can be said?'

Mr Jones gave himself up to reflection for a few moments before he replied to this. He supposed that he was bound to believe the story as far as it went. At any rate, he did not know how he could say that he did not believe it. It seemed to him to be almost incredible, – especially incredible in regard to that personal mistake, for, except that they both had long beards and brown beards, Mr Jones thought that there was no point of resemblance between himself and Mr Brown. But still, even that, he felt, must be accepted. But then why had he been left, deserted, to undergo all those torments? 'She found out her mistake at last, I suppose?' he said.

'Oh, yes.'

'Why didn't she wake a fellow and take it off again?'

'Ah!'

'She can't have cared very much for a man's comfort when she went away and left him like that.'

'Ah! there was the difficulty, Mr Jones.'

'Difficulty! Who was it that had done it? To come to me, in my bedroom, in the middle of the night and put that thing on me, and then leave it there and say nothing about it! It seems to me deuced like a practical joke.'

'No, Mr Jones!'

'That's the way I look at it,' said Mr Jones, plucking up his courage.

'There isn't a woman in all England, or in all France, less likely to do such a thing than my wife. She's as steady as a rock, Mr Jones, and would no more go into another gentleman's bedroom in joke than — Oh dear no! You're going to be a married man yourself.'

'Unless all this makes a difference,' said Mr Jones, almost in tears. 'I had sworn that I would be with her this Christmas Eve.'

'Oh, Mr Jones, I cannot believe that will interfere with your happiness. How could you think that your wife, as is to be, would do such a thing as that in joke?'

'She wouldn't do it at all; — joke or anyway.'

'How can you tell what accident might happen to any one?'

'She'd have wakened the man then afterwards. I'm sure she would. She would never have left him to suffer in that way. Her heart is too soft. Why didn't she send you to wake me, and explain it all. That's what my Jane would have done; and I should have gone and wakened him. But the whole thing is impossible,' he said, shaking his head as he remembered that he and his Jane were not in a condition as yet to undergo any such mutual trouble. At last Mr Jones was brought to acknowledge that nothing more could be done. The lady sent her apology, and told her story, and he must bear the trouble and inconvenience to which she had subjected him. He still, however, had his own opinion about her conduct generally, and could not be brought to give any sign of amity. He simply bowed when Mr Brown was hoping to induce him to shake hands, and sent no word of pardon to the great offender.

The matter, however, was so far concluded that there was no further question of police interference, nor any doubt but that the lady with her husband was to be allowed to leave Paris by the night train. The nature of the accident probably became known to all. Mr Brown was interrogated by many, and though he professed to declare that he would answer no question, nevertheless he found it better to tell the clerk something of the truth than to allow the matter to be shrouded in mystery. It is to be feared that Mr Jones, who did not once show himself through the day, but who employed the hours in endeavouring to assuage the injury done him, still lived in the conviction that the lady had played a practical joke on him. But the subject of such a joke never talks about it, and Mr Jones could not be induced to speak even by friendly adherence of the night-porter.

Mrs Brown also clung to the seclusion of her own bedroom, never once stirring from it till the time came in which she was to be taken down to the omnibus. Upstairs she ate her meals, and upstairs she passed her time in packing and unpacking, and in requesting that telegrams might be sent repeatedly to Thompson Hall. In the course of the day two such telegrams were sent, in the latter of which the Thompson family were assured that the Browns would arrive, probably in time for breakfast on Christmas

Day, certainly in time for church. She asked more than once tenderly after Mr Jones' welfare, but could obtain no information. 'He was very cross, and that's all I know about it,' said Mr Brown. Then she made a remark as to the gentleman's Christian name, which appeared on the card as 'Barnaby.' 'My sister's husband's name will be Burnaby,' she said. 'And this man's Christian name is Barnaby; that's all the difference,' said her husband, with ill-timed jocularity.

We all know how people under a cloud are apt to fail in asserting their personal dignity. On the former day a separate vehicle had been ordered by Mr Brown to take himself and his wife to the station, but now, after his misfortunes, he contented himself with such provision as the people at the hotel might make for him. At the appointed hour he brought his wife down, thickly veiled. There were many strangers as she passed through the hall, ready to look at the lady who had done that wonderful thing in the dead of night, but none could see a feature of her face as she stepped across the hall, and was hurried into the omnibus. And there were many eyes also on Mr Jones, who followed her very quickly, for he also, in spite of his sufferings, was leaving Paris on the evening in order that he might be with his English friends on Christmas Day. He, as he went through the crowd, assumed an air of great dignity, to which, perhaps, something was added by his endeavours, as he walked, to save his poor throat from irritation. He, too, got into the same omnibus, stumbling over the feet of his enemy in the dark. At the station they got their tickets, one close after the other, and then were brought into each other's presence in the waiting-room. I think it must be acknowledged that here Mr Jones was conscious not only of her presence, but of her consciousness of his presence, and that he assumed an attitude, as though he should have said, 'Now do you think it possible for me to believe that you mistook me for your husband?' She was perfectly quiet, but sat through that quarter of an hour with her face continually veiled. Mr Brown made some little overture of conversation to Mr Jones, but Mr Jones, though he did mutter some reply, showed plainly enough that he had no desire for further intercourse. Then came the accustomed stampede, the awful rush, the internecine struggle in which seats had to be found. Seats, I fancy, are regularly found, even by the most tardy, but it always appears that every British father and every British husband is actuated at these stormy moments by a conviction that unless he prove himself a very Hercules he and his daughters and his wife will be left desolate in Paris. Mr Brown was quite Herculean, carrying two bags and a hat-box in his own hands, besides the cloaks, the coats, the rugs, the sticks, and the umbrellas. But when he had got himself and his wife well seated, with their faces to the engine, with a corner seat for her, – there was Mr Jones immediately opposite to her. Mr Jones, as soon as he perceived the inconvenience of his position, made a scramble for another place, but he was too late. In that contiguity the journey as far as Dover had to be made. She, poor woman, never once took up her veil. There he sat, without closing an eye, stiff as a ramrod, sometimes showing by little uneasy gestures that the trouble at his neck was still there, but never speaking a word, and hardly moving a limb.

Crossing from Calais to Dover the lady was, of course, separated from her victim. The passage was very bad, and she more than once reminded her husband how well it would have been with them now had they pursued their journey as she had intended, – as though they had been detained in Paris by his fault! Mr Jones, as he laid himself down on his back, gave himself up to wondering whether any man before him had ever been made subject to such absolute injustice. Now and again he put his hand up to his own beard, and began to doubt whether it could have been moved, as it must have been moved, without waking him. What if chloroform had been used? Many such suspicions crossed his mind during the misery of that passage.

They were again together in the same railway carriage from Dover to London. They had now got used to the close neighbourhood, and knew how to endure each the presence of the other. But as yet Mr Jones had never seen the lady's face. He longed to know what were the features of the woman who had been so blind – if indeed that story were true. Or if it were not true, of what like was the woman who would dare in the middle of the night to play such a trick as that. But still she kept her veil close over her face.

From Cannon Street the Browns took their departure in a cab for the Liverpool Street Station, whence they would be conveyed by the Eastern Counties Railway to Stratford. Now at any rate their troubles were over. They would be in ample time, not only for Christmas Day church, but for Christmas Day breakfast. 'It will be just the same as getting in there last night,' said Mr Brown, as he walked across the platform to place his wife in the carriage for Stratford. She entered it first, and as she did so there she saw Mr Jones seated in the corner! Hitherto she had borne his presence well, but now she could not restrain herself from a little start and a little scream. He bowed his head very slightly, as though acknowledging the compliment, and then down she dropped her veil. When they arrived at Stratford, the journey being over in a quarter of an hour, Jones was out of the carriage even before the Browns.

'There is Uncle John's carriage,' said Mrs Brown, thinking that now, at any rate, she would be able to free herself from the presence of this terrible stranger. No doubt he was a handsome man to look at, but on no face so sternly hostile had she ever before fixed her eyes. She did not, perhaps, reflect diat the owner of no other face had ever been so deeply injured by herself.

MRS BROWN AT THOMPSON HALL

'Please, sir, we were to ask for Mr Jones,' said the servant, putting his head into the carriage after both Mr and Mrs Brown had seated themselves.

'Mr Jones!' exclaimed the husband.

'Why ask for Mr Jones?' demanded the wife. The servant was about to tender some explanation when Mr Jones stepped up and said that he was Mr Jones. 'We are going to Thompson Hall,' said the lady with great vigour.

'So am I,' said Mr Jones, with much dignity. It was, however, arranged that he should sit with the coachman, as there was a rumble behind for the other servant. The luggage was put into a cart, and away all went for Thompson Hall.

'What do you think about it, Mary,' whispered Mr Brown, after a pause. He was evidently awe-struck by the horror of the occasion.

'I cannot make it out at all. What do you think?'

'I don't know what to think. Jones going to Thompson Hall!'

'He's a very good-looking young man,' said Mrs Brown.

'Well; – that's as people think. A stiff, stuck-up fellow, I should say. Up to this moment he has never forgiven you for what you did to him.'

'Would you have forgiven his wife, Charles, if she'd done it to you?'

'He hasn't got a wife, – yet.'

'How do you know?'

'He is coming home now to be married,' said Mr Brown. 'He expects to meet the young lady this very Christmas Day. He told me so. That was one of the reasons why he was so angry at being stopped by what you did last night.'

'I suppose he knows Uncle John, or he wouldn't be going to the Hall,' said Mrs Brown.

'I can't make it out,' said Mr Brown, shaking his head.

'He looks quite like a gentleman,' said Mrs Brown, 'though he has been so stiff. Jones! Barnaby Jones! You're sure it was Barnaby?'

'That was the name on the card.'

'Not Burnaby?' asked Mrs. Brown.

'It was Barnaby Jones on the card, – just the same as "Barnaby Rudge," and as for looking like a gentleman, I'm by no means quite so sure. A gentleman takes an apology when it's offered.'

'Perhaps, my dear, that depends on the condition of his throat. If you had had a mustard plaster on all night, you might not have liked it. But here we are at Thompson Hall at last.'

Thompson Hall was an old brick mansion, standing within a huge iron gate, with a gravel sweep before it. It had stood there before Stratford was a town, or even a suburb, and had then been known by the name Bow Place. But it had been in the hands of the present family for the last thirty years, and was now known far and wide as Thompson Hall, – a comfortable, roomy, old-fashioned place, perhaps a little dark and dull to look at, but much more substantially built than most of our modern villas. Mrs Brown jumped with alacrity from the carriage, and with a quick step entered the home of her forefathers. Her husband followed her more leisurely, but he, too, felt that he was at home at Thompson Hall. Then Mr Jones walked in also; – but he looked as though he were not at all at home. It was still very early, and no one of the family was as yet down. In these circumstances it was almost necessary that something should be said to Mr Jones.

'Do you know Mr Thompson?' asked Mr Brown.

'I never had the pleasure of seeing him, – as yet,' answered Mr Jones, very stiffly.

'Oh, – I didn't know; – because you said you were coming here.'

'And I have come here. Are you friends of Mr Thompson?'

'Oh, dear, yes,' said Mrs Brown. 'I was a Thompson myself before I married.'

'Oh, – indeed!' said Mr Jones. 'How very odd; – very odd indeed.'

During this time the luggage was being brought into the house, and two old family servants were offering them assistance. Would the new comers like to go up to their bedrooms? Then the housekeeper, Mrs Green, intimated with a wink that Miss Jane would, she was sure, be down quite immediately. The present moment, however, was still very unpleasant. The lady probably had made her guess as to the mystery; but the two gentlemen were still altogether in the dark. Mrs Brown had no doubt declared her parentage, but Mr Jones, with such a multitude of strange facts crowding on his mind, had been slow to understand her. Being some what suspicious by nature he was beginning to think whether possibly the mustard had been put by this lady on his throat with some reference to his connexion with Thompson Hall. Could it be that she, for some reason of her own, had wished to prevent his coming, and had contrived this untoward stratagem out of her brain? or had she wished to make him ridiculous to the Thompson family, – to whom, as a family, he was at present unknown? It was becoming more and more improbable to him that the whole thing should have been an accident. When, after the first horrid torments of that morning in which he had in his agony invoked the assistance of the night-porter, he had begun to reflect on his situation, he had determined that it would be better that nothing further should be said about it. What would life be worth to him if he were to be known wherever he went as the man who had been mustard-plastered in the middle of the night by a strange lady? The worst of a practical joke is that the remembrance of the absurd condition sticks so long to the sufferer! At the hotel that night-porter, who had possessed himself of the handkerchief and had read the name and had connected that name with the occupant of 333 whom he had found wandering about the house with some strange purpose, had not permitted the thing to sleep. The porter had pressed the matter home against the Browns, and had produced the interview which has been recorded. But during the whole of that day Mr. Jones had been resolving that he would never again either think of the Browns or speak of them. A great injury had been done to him, – a most outrageous injustice; – but it was a thing which had to be endured. A horrid woman had come across him like a nightmare. All he could do was to endeavour to forget the terrible visitation. Such had been his resolve, – in making which he had passed that long day in Paris. And now the Browns had stuck to him from the moment of his leaving his room! He had been forced to travel with them, but had travelled with them as a stranger. He had tried to comfort himself with the reflection that at every fresh stage he would shake them off. In one railway after another the vicinity had been bad, – but still they were strangers. Now he found himself in the same house with them, – where of course the story would be told. Had not the thing been done on purpose that the story might be told there at Thompson Hall?

Mrs Brown had acceded to the proposition of the housekeeper, and was about to be taken to her room when there was heard a sound of footsteps along the passage above and on the stairs, and a young lady came bounding on to the scene. 'You have all of you come a quarter of an hour earlier than we thought possible,' said the young lady. 'I did so mean to be up to receive you!' With that she passed her sister on the stairs, – for the young lady was Miss Jane Thompson, sister to our Mrs Brown, – and hurried down into the hall. Here Mr Brown, who had ever been on affectionate terms with his sister-in-law, put himself forward to receive her embraces; but she, apparently not noticing him in her ardour, rushed on and threw herself on to the breast of the other gentleman. 'This is my Charles,' she said. 'Oh, Charles, I thought you never would be here.'

Mr Charles Burnaby Jones, for such was his name since he had inherited the Jones property in Pembrokeshire, received into his arms the ardent girl of his heart with all that love, and devotion to which she was entitled, but could not do so without some external shrinking from her embrace. 'Oh, Charles, what is it?' she said.

'Nothing, dearest – only – only– .' Then he looked piteously up into Mrs Brown's face, as though imploring her not to tell the story.

'Perhaps, Jane, you had better introduce us,' said Mrs Brown.

'Introduce you! I thought you had been travelling together, and staying at the same hotel – and all that.'

'So we have; but people may be in the same hotel without knowing each other. And we have travelled all the way home with Mr Jones without in the least knowing who he was.'

'How very odd! Do you mean you have never spoken?'

'Not a word,' said Mrs Brown.

'I do so hope you'll love each other,' said Jane.

'It shan't be my fault if we don't,' said Mrs Brown.

'I'm sure it shan't be mine,' said Mr Brown, tendering his hand to the other gentleman. The various feelings of the moment were too much for Mr Jones, and he could not respond quite as he should have done. But as he was taken upstairs to his room he determined that he would make the best of it.

The owner of the house was old Uncle John. He was a bachelor, and with him lived various members of the family. There was the great Thompson of them all, Cousin Robert, who was now member of Parliament for the Essex Flats, and young John, as a certain enterprising Thompson of the age of forty was usually called, and then there was old Aunt Bess, and among other young branches there was Miss Jane Thompson who was now engaged to marry Mr Charles Burnaby Jones. As it happened, no other member of the family had as yet seen Mr Burnaby Jones, and he, being by nature of a retiring disposition, felt himself to be ill at ease when he came into the breakfast-parlour among all the Thompsons. He was known to be a gentleman of good family and ample means, and all the Thompsons had approved of the match, but during that first Christmas breakfast he did not seem to accept his condition jovially. His own Jane sat beside him, but then on the other side sat Mrs Brown. She assumed an immediate intimacy, – as women know how to do on such occasions, – being determined from the very first to regard her sister's husband as a brother; but he still feared her. She was still to him the woman who had come to him in the dead of night with that horrid mixture, – and had then left him.

'It was so odd that both of you should have been detained on the very same day,' said Jane.

'Yes, it was odd,' said Mrs Brown, with a smile, looking round upon her neighbour.

'It was abominably bad weather, you know,' said Brown.

'But you were both so determined to come,' said the old gentleman. 'When we got the two telegrams at the same moment, we were sure that there had been some agreement between you.'

'Not exactly an agreement,' said Mrs Brown; whereupon Mr Jones looked as grim as death.

'I'm sure there is something more than we understand yet,' said the member of Parliament.

Then they all went to church, as a united family ought to do on Christmas Day, and came home to a fine old English early dinner at three o'clock, – a sirloin of beef a foot-and-a-half broad, a turkey as big as an ostrich, a plum-pudding bigger than the turkey, and two or three dozen mince-pies. 'That's a very large bit of beef,' said Mr Jones, who had not lived much in England latterly. 'It won't look so large,' said the old gentleman, 'when all our friends downstairs have had their say to it.' 'A plum-pudding on Christmas Day can't be too big,' he said again, 'if the cook will but take time enough over it. I never knew a bit go to waste yet.'

By this time there had been some explanation as to past events between the two sisters. Mrs Brown had indeed told Jane all about it, how ill her husband had been, how she had been forced to go down and look for the mustard, and then what she had done with the mustard. 'I don't think they are a bit alike you know, Mary, if you mean that,' said Jane.

'Well, no; perhaps not quite alike. I only saw his beard, you know. No doubt it was stupid, but I did it.'

'Why didn't you take it off again?' asked the sister.

'Oh, Jane, if you'd only think of it? Could you!' Then of course all that occurred was explained, how they had been stopped on their journey, how Brown had made the best apology in his power, and how Jones had travelled with them and had never spoken a word. The gentleman had only taken his new name a week since but of course had had his new card printed immediately. 'I'm sure I should have thought of it if they hadn't made a mistake with the first name. Charles said it was like Barnaby Rudge.'

'Not at all like Barnaby Rudge,' said Jane; 'Charles Burnaby Jones is a very good name.'

'Very good indeed, – and I'm sure that after a little bit he won't be at all the worse for the accident.'

Before dinner the secret had been told no further, but still there had crept about among the Thompsons, and, indeed, downstairs also, among the retainers, a feeling that there was a secret. The old housekeeper was sure that Miss Mary, as she still called Mrs Brown, had something to tell if she could only be induced to tell it, and that this something had reference to Mr Jones' personal comfort. The head of the family, who was a sharp old gentleman, felt this also, and the member of Parliament, who had an idea that he specially should never be kept in the dark, was almost angry. Mr Jones, suffering from some kindred feeling throughout the dinner, remained silent and unhappy. When two or three toasts had been drunk, – the Queen's health, the old gentleman's health, the young couple's health, Brown's health, and the general health of all the Thompsons, then tongues were loosened and a question was asked, 'I know that there has been something doing in Paris between these young people that we haven't heard as yet,' said the uncle. Then Mrs Brown laughed, and Jane, laughing too, gave Mr Jones to understand that she at any rate knew all about it.

'If there is a mystery I hope it will be told at once,' said the member of Parliament, angrily.

'Come, Brown, what is it?' asked another male cousin.

'Well, there was an accident. I'd rather Jones should tell,' said he.

Jones' brow became blacker than thunder, but he did not say a word. 'You mustn't be angry with Mary,' Jane whispered into her lover's ear.

'Come, Mary, you never were slow at talking,' said the uncle.

'I do hate this kind of thing,' said the member of Parliament.

'I will tell it all,' said Mrs Brown, very nearly in tears, or else pretending to be very nearly in tears. 'I know I was very wrong, and I do beg his pardon, and if he won't say that he forgives me I never shall be happy again.' Then she clasped her hands, and, turning round, looked him piteously in the face.

'Oh yes; I do forgive you,' said Mr Jones.

'My brother,' said she, throwing her arms round him and kissing him. He recoiled from the embrace, but I think that he attempted to return the kiss. 'And now I will tell the whole story,' said Mrs Brown. And she told it, acknowledging her fault with true contrition, and swearing that she would atone for it by life-long sisterly devotion.

'And you mustard-plastered the wrong man!' said the old gentleman, almost rolling off his chair with delight.

'I did,' said Mrs. Brown, sobbing, 'and I think that no woman ever suffered as I suffered.'

'And Jones wouldn't let you leave the hotel?'

'It was the handkerchief stopped us,' said Brown.

'If it had turned out to be anybody else,' said the member of Parliament, 'the results might have been most serious, – not to say discreditable.'

'That's nonsense, Robert,' said Mrs Brown, who was disposed to resent the use of so severe a word, even from the legislator cousin.

'In a strange gentleman's bedroom!' he continued. 'It only shows that what I have always said is quite true. You should never go to bed in a strange house without locking your door.'

Nevertheless it was a very jovial meeting, and before the evening was over Mr Jones was happy, and had been brought to acknowledge that the mustard plaster would probably not do him any permanent injury.

'Christmas Shopping' from *The Green Road* by Anne Enright

Anne Enright is one of Ireland's most celebrated writers and the current Laureate for Irish Fiction. She was born and raised in Dublin, the city where she now lives. She writes articles, essays and short stories but is most famous for her novels, in particular *The Gathering*, which won the Man Booker Prize in 2007, and her most recent, the critically acclaimed *The Green Road*.

In this extract from *The Green Road*, Constance prepares for a final Christmas at Ardeevin, her mother Rosaleen's home, which is about to be sold. Constance's family – her husband Dessie and children – are gathering along with her siblings, Dan, Hanna and Emmet.

Read more by Anne Enright:

The Green Road

The Gathering

The Forgotten Waltz

Rosaleen told Constance she did not want a present this year. She said it in a faint voice, meaning she would be dead soon so what was the point? What was an object – when you would not have it for long? Too much? Not enough? It was hard to say.

Constance thought she was immune to this sort of guff, but she also needed to tell her mother that she was not about to die so she went up to Galway and trawled through every last thing in the shops, until she found a thick silk scarf that was the same price as a new microwave and so beautiful you could not say what colour it was, except there was lilac in there and also pearl, all of which would be perfect for her mother's complexion and for her silver-white hair.

'Oh I can't remember,' she would say when her mother asked the price, or complained about the price. Times were good. Constance bought a wheel of Camembert, various boxes of chocolates, Parma ham and beautiful, small grapes that were more yellow than green. She got her hair done in a place so posh it didn't look done at all. Then she drove back home through the winter darkness in the smell of PVC and ripening cheese, happy in her car. Constance loved to drive. It was the perfect excuse. For what, she did not know. But there was such simplicity to it: crossing great distances to stop an inch away from the kerb, opening the door.

The next morning she was back behind the wheel, picking Dan up from the airport, depositing him in her mother's, back in to the butcher's and a few things around town, a poinsettia for the cleaner, a trio of hyacinths for the cleaner's mother who was in hospital in Limerick and could not understand a thing the doctors told her. The cleaner was from Mongolia, a fact that made Constance slightly dizzy. But it was just true. Her cleaner – good hearted, a little bit vague with a duster – was from Ulan Bator. Constance left the presents with her money on the kitchen table, then back out to Ardeevin with the turkey and a quick tidy up while she was there: checking supplies, running a Hoover, though her mother hated the sound of the Hoover. After which, home to drive Shauna to a pal's house, her fake tan leaving a shadow on the cream upholstery of the Lexus.

'Ooofff,' said Constance, when she saw it and then chastised her temper. That all her problems should be so small.

The next morning, she went early into Ennis. It was 10 a.m. on Christmas Eve and the supermarket was like the Apocalypse, people grabbing without looking, and things fallen in the aisles. But there was no good time to do this, you just had to get through it. Constance pushed her trolley to the vegetable section: celery, carrots, parsnips for Dessie, who liked them. Sausage and sage for the stuffing, an experimental bag of chestnuts, vacuum packed. Constance bought a case of Prosecco on special offer to wrap and leave on various doorsteps and threw in eight frozen pizzas in case the kids rolled up with friends. Frozen berries. Different ice cream. She got wine, sherry, whiskey, fresh nuts, salted nuts, crisps, bags and bags of apples, two mangoes, a melon, dark cherries for the fruit salad, root ginger, fresh mint, a wooden crate of satsumas, the fruit cold and promising sweet, each one with its own sprig of green, dark leaves. She got wrapping paper, red paper napkins, Sellotape, and – more out of habit, now the children were grown – packs and packs of batteries, triple A, double A, a few Cs. She took five squat candles in cream-coloured beeswax to fill the cracked hearth in the good room at Ardeevin, where no fire was lit this ten years past, and two long rolls of simple red baubles to fill the gaps on her mother's tree. She went back for more sausages because she had forgotten about breakfast. Tomatoes. Bacon. Eggs. She went back to the dairy section for more cheese. Back to the fruit aisle for seedless grapes. Back to the biscuit aisle for water biscuits. She searched high and low for string to keep the cloth on the pudding, stopped at the delicatessen counter for pesto, chicken liver pâté, tubs of olives. She got some ready-cooked drumsticks to keep people going. At every corner, she met a neighbour, an old friend, they rolled their eyes and threw Christmas greetings, and no one thought her rude for not stopping to converse. She smiled at a baby in the queue for the till.

'I know!' she said. 'Yes I know!' The baby considered her fully. The baby gave her a look that was complete.

'Yes!' she said again, and got the curl of a sweet, thoughtful smile.

All this kept Constance occupied until the time came to unload the contents of her trolley on to the conveyor. The baby held itself so proudly erect, the young mother underneath it looked like a prop. She looked like some kind of clapped-out baby stand.

'You're doing great,' Constance told her. 'You're doing a great job.'

The bill came to four hundred and ten euros, a new record. She thought she should keep the receipt for posterity. Dessie would be almost proud.

Constance pushed her trolley on to the walkway and the wheels locked cleverly on to the metal beneath them, and she was happy happy happy, as she sank towards the car park. She thanked God from the burning, rising depth of herself for this unexpected life – a man who loved her, two sons taller than their father, and a daughter who kissed her still when no one was there to see. She could not believe this was the way things had turned out.

Her feet were swollen already; she could feel them throb, hot in the wrong shoes. Constance bumped the trolley off the walkway, set her trotters thumping across the concrete of the car park. It was half past eleven on Christmas Eve. In the pocket of her coat, her phone started to ring and, by the telepathy of the timing, Constance knew it was her mother.

'What is it, darling,' she said, remembering, as she did so, that she had forgotten the Brussels sprouts.

'He's still asleep,' said Rosaleen. For a moment Constance thought she was talking about her father, a man who was not asleep, but dead.

'Well don't wake him,' she said.

Dan. Of course, she meant Dan, who was jet lagged.

'Should I?'

'Or maybe do. Yeah. Get him straightened out.'

There was a pause from Rosaleen. *Straightened out.*

'You think?'

'Have you everything?' said Constance.

'I don't know,' said her mother.

'Don't worry.'

'It's a lot of work,' Rosaleen said, with a real despair in her voice; you would think she had just spent an hour in the insanity of the supermarket, not Constance. 'But I suppose it's worth it to have you all here.'

'I suppose.'

'I'll be sorry to see it go.' She was talking about the house again. Any time she felt needy, now, or lost or uncertain, she talked about the house.

'Right,' said Constance. 'Listen, Mammy.'

'*Mammy*,' said Rosaleen.

'Listen –'

'Oh, don't bother. I'll let you go.' And she was gone.

It was Rosaleen, of course, who wanted Brussels sprouts, no one else ate them. Constance stood for a moment, blank behind the crammed boot of the Lexus. You can't have Christmas without Brussels sprouts.

Sometimes even Rosaleen left them on her plate. Something to do with cruciferous vegetables, or nightshades, because even vegetables were poison to her when the wind was from the north-east.

'Oh what the hell,' said Constance. She slammed the boot shut and turned her sore feet back to the walkway and the horrors of the vegetable section. Then over to the spices to get nutmeg, which was the way Rosaleen liked her Brussels, with unsalted butter. And it was a good thing she went back up, because she had no cranberry sauce either – unbelievably – no brandy for the brandy butter, no honey to glaze the ham. It was as though she had thrown the whole shop in the trolley and bought nothing. She had no big foil for the turkey. Constance grabbed some potato salad, coleslaw, smoked salmon, mayonnaise, more tomatoes, litre bottles of fizzy drinks for the kids, kitchen roll, cling film, extra toilet paper, extra bin bags. She didn't even look at the bill after another fifteen minutes in the queue behind some woman who had forgotten flowers – as she announced – and abandoned her groceries to get them, after which Constance did exactly the same thing, fetching two bouquets of strong pink lilies because they had no white left. She was on the way home before she remembered potatoes, thought about pulling over to the side of the road and digging some out of a field, imagined herself with her hands in the earth, scrabbling around for a few spuds.

Lifting her head to howl.

Back in Aughavanna she unpacked and sorted the stuff that would go over to Ardeevin for the Christmas dinner and she repacked that. Then she went to Rory's room, where the child was sleeping off a hangover. Constance took off her shoes and climbed on to the bed behind him.

'Oh fuck,' he said.

'Your own fault,' said his mother, as she spooned into him, with the duvet between them and the wall at her back.

'Ah, Ma,' he said and flapped a big hand over his shoulder to find a bit of her, which happened to be the top of her head. But Rory was always easy to hold; easy to carry and easy to kiss, and there, in the smell of last night's beer and his rude good health, fretful, lumpy Constance McGrath fell asleep.

'A Conscience Pudding' from
The New Treasure Seekers by E. Nesbit

Edith Nesbit was born in 1858. Her father died when she was only three and her impoverished family moved continually all over England. As young married woman with small children, she sold stories and poems to supplement the family income. Her first children's book, *The Treasure Seekers*, was published in 1899. She also wrote *Five Children and It* but her most famous story, *The Railway Children*, was first published in 1905 and has never been out of print. Edith Nesbit died in 1924.

Read more by E. Nesbit:
Five Children and It
The Phoenix and the Carpet
The Railway Children

It was Christmas, nearly a year after Mother died. I cannot write about Mother – but I will just say one thing. If she had only been away for a little while, and not for always, we shouldn't have been so keen on having a Christmas. I didn't understand this then, but I am much older now, and I think it was just because everything was so different and horrid we felt we *must* do something; and perhaps we were not particular enough *what*. Things make you much more unhappy when you loaf about than when you are doing events.

Father had to go away just about Christmas. He had heard that his wicked partner, who ran away with his money, was in France, and he thought he could catch him, but really he was in Spain, where catching criminals is never practised. We did not know this till afterwards.

Before Father went away he took Dora and Oswald into his study, and said –

'I'm awfully sorry I've got to go away, but it is very serious business, and I must go. You'll be good while I'm away, kiddies, won't you?'

We promised faithfully. Then he said –

'There are reasons – you wouldn't understand if I tried to tell you – but you can't have much of a Christmas this year. But I've told Matilda to make you a good plain pudding. Perhaps next Christmas will be brighter.'

(It was; for the next Christmas saw us the affluent nephews and nieces of an Indian uncle – but that is quite another story, as good old Kipling says.)

When Father had been seen off at Lewisham Station with his bags, and a plaid rug in a strap, we came home again, and it was horrid. There were papers and things littered all over his room where he had packed. We tidied the room up – it was the only thing we could do for him. It was Dicky who accidentally broke his shaving-glass, and H.O. made a paper boat out of a letter we found out afterwards Father particularly wanted to keep. This took us some time, and when we went into the nursery the fire was black out, and we could not get it alight again, even with the whole *Daily Chronicle*. Matilda, who was our general then, was out, as well as the fire, so we went and sat in the kitchen. There is always a good fire in kitchens. The kitchen hearthrug was not nice to sit on, so we spread newspapers on it.

It was sitting in the kitchen, I think, that brought to our minds my Father's parting words – about the pudding, I mean.

Oswald said, 'Father said we couldn't have much of a Christmas for secret reasons, and he said he had told Matilda to make us a plain pudding.'

The plain pudding instantly cast its shadow over the deepening gloom of our young minds.

'I wonder *how* plain she'll make it?' Dicky said.

'As plain as plain, you may depend,' said Oswald. 'A here-am-I-where-are-you pudding – that's her sort.'

The others groaned, and we gathered closer round the fire till the newspapers rustled madly.

'I believe I could make a pudding that *wasn't* plain, if I tried,' Alice said. 'Why shouldn't we?'

'No chink,' said Oswald, with brief sadness.

'How much would it cost?' Noël asked, and added that Dora had twopence and H.O. had a French halfpenny.

Dora got the cookery-book out of the dresser drawer, where it lay doubled up among clothes-pegs, dirty dusters, scallop shells, string, penny novelettes, and the dining-room corkscrew. The general we had then – it seemed as if she did all the cooking on the cookery-book instead of on the baking-board, there were traces of so many bygone meals upon its pages.

'It doesn't say Christmas pudding at all,' said Dora.

'Try plum,' the resourceful Oswald instantly counselled.

Dora turned the greasy pages anxiously.

'"Plum-pudding, 518.

'"A rich, with flour, 517.

'"Christmas, 517.

'"Cold brandy sauce for, 241."

'We shouldn't care about that, so it's no use looking.

'"Good without eggs, 518.

'"Plain, 518."

'We don't want *that* anyhow. "Christmas, 517" – that's the one.'

It took her a long time to find page. Oswald got a shovel of coals and made up the fine. It blazed up like the devouring elephant the *Daily Telegraph* always calls it. Then Dora read –

'"Christmas plum-pudding. Time six hours."'

'To eat it in?' said H.O.

'No, silly! To make it.'

'Forge ahead, Dora,' Dicky replied.

Dora went on –

'"2072. One pound and a half of raisins; half a pound of currants; three-quarters of a pound of breadcrumbs; half a pound of flour; three-quarters of a pound of beef suet; nine eggs; one wineglassful of brandy; half a pound of citron and orange peel; half a nutmeg; and a little ground ginger." I wonder *how* little ground ginger.'

'A teacupful would be enough, I think,' Alice said; 'we must not be extravagant.'

'We haven't got anything yet to be extravagant *with*,' said Oswald, who had toothache that day. 'What would you do with the things if you'd got them?'

'You'd "chop the suet as fine as possible" – I wonder how fine that is?' replied Dora and the book together – '"and mix it with the breadcrumbs and flour; add the currants washed and dried."'

'Not starched, then,' said Alice.

'"The citron and orange peel cut into thin slices" – I wonder what they call thin? Matilda's thin bread-and-butter is quite different from what I mean by it – "and the raisins stoned and divided." How many heaps would you divide them into?'

'Seven, I suppose,' said Alice; 'one for each person and one for the pot – I mean pudding.'

'"Mix it all well together with the grated nutmeg and ginger. Then stir in nine eggs well beaten, and the brandy" – we'll leave that out, I think – "and again mix it thoroughly together that every ingredient may be moistened; put it into a buttered mould, tie over tightly, and boil for six hours. Serve it ornamented with holly and brandy poured over it."'

'I should think holly and brandy poured over it would be simply beastly,' said Dicky.

'I expect the book knows. I daresay holly and water would do as well though. "This pudding may be made a month before" – it's no use reading about that though, because we've only got four days to Christmas.'

'It's no use reading about any of it,' said Oswald, with thoughtful repeatedness, 'because we haven't got the things, and we haven't got the coin to get them.'

'We might get the tin somehow,' said Dicky.

'There must be lots of kind people who would subscribe to a Christmas pudding for poor children who hadn't any,' Noël said.

'Well, I'm going skating at Penn's,' said Oswald. 'It's no use thinking about puddings. We must put up with it plain.'

So he went, and Dicky went with him.

When they returned to their home in the evening the fire had been lighted again in the nursery, and the others were just having tea. We toasted our bread-and-butter on the bare side, and it gets a little warm among the butter. This is called French toast. 'I like English better, but it is more expensive,' Alice said –

'Matilda is in a frightful rage about your putting those coals on the kitchen fire, Oswald. She says we shan't have enough to last over Christmas as it is. And Father gave her a talking to before he went about them – asked her if she ate them, she says – but I don't believe he did. Anyway, she's locked the coal-cellar door, and she's got the key in her pocket. I don't see how we can boil the pudding.'

'What pudding?' said Oswald dreamily. He was thinking of a chap he had seen at Penn's who had cut the date 1899 on the ice with four strokes.

'*The* pudding,' Alice said. 'Oh, we've had such a time, Oswald! First Dora and I went to the shops to find out exactly what the pudding would cost – it's only two-and-elevenpence halfpenny, counting in the holly.'

'It's no good,' Oswald repeated; he is very patient and will say the same thing any number of times. 'It's no good. You know we've got no tin.'

'Ah,' said Alice, 'but Noël and I went out, and we called at some of the houses in Granville Park and Dartmouth Hill – and we got a lot of sixpences and shillings, besides pennies, and one old gentleman gave us half-a-crown. He was so nice. Quite bald, with a knitted red and blue waistcoat. We 've got eight-and-sevenpence.'

Oswald did not feel quite sure Father would like us to go asking for shillings and sixpences, or even half-crowns from strangers, but he did not say so. The money had been asked for and got, and it couldn't be helped – and perhaps he wanted the pudding – I am not able to remember exactly why he did not speak up and say, 'This is wrong,' but anyway he didn't.

Alice and Dora went out and bought the things next morning. They bought double quantities, so that it came to five shillings and elevenpence, and was enough to make a noble pudding. There was a lot of holly left over for decorations. We used very little for the sauce. The money that was left we spent very anxiously in other things to eat, such as dates and figs and toffee.

We did not tell Matilda about it. She was a red-haired girl, and apt to turn shirty at the least thing.

Concealed under our jackets and overcoats we carried the parcels up to the nursery, and hid them in the treasure-chest we had there. It was the bureau drawer. It was locked up afterwards because the treacle got all over the green baize and the little drawers inside it while we were waiting to begin to make the pudding. It was the grocer told us we ought to put treacle in the pudding, and also about not so much ginger as a teacupful.

When Matilda had begun to pretend to scrub the floor (she pretended this three times a week so as to have an excuse not to let us in the kitchen, but I know she used to read novelettes most of the time, because Alice and I had a squint through the window more than once), we barricaded the nursery door and set to work. We were very careful to be quite clean. We washed our hands as well as the currants. I have sometimes thought we did not get all the soap off the currants. The pudding smelt like a washing-day when the time came to cut it open. And we washed a corner of the table to chop the suet on. Chopping suet looks easy till you try.

Father's machine he weighs letters with did to weigh out the things. We did this very carefully, in case the grocer had not done so. Everything was right except the raisins. H.O. had carried them home. He was very young then, and there was a hole in the corner of the paper bag and his mouth was sticky.

Lots of people have been hanged to a gibbet in chains on evidence no worse than that, and we told H.O. so till he cried. This was good for him. It was not unkindness to H.O., but part of our duty.

Chopping suet as fine as possible is much harder than any one would think, as I said before. So is crumbling bread – especially if your loaf is new, like ours was. When we had done them the breadcrumbs and the suet were both very large and lumpy, and of a dingy grey colour, something like pale slate pencil.

They looked a better colour when we had mixed them with the flour. The girls had washed the currants with Brown Windsor soap and the sponge. Some of the currants got inside the sponge and kept coming out in the bath for days afterwards. I see now that this was not quite nice. We cut the candied peel as thin as we wish people would cut our bread-and-butter. We tried to take the stones out of the raisins, but they were too sticky, so we just divided them up in seven lots. Then we mixed the other things in the wash-hand basin from the spare bedroom that was always spare. We each put in our own lot of raisins and turned it all into a pudding-basin, and tied it up in one of Alice's pinafores, which was the nearest thing to a proper pudding-cloth we could find – at any rate clean. What was left sticking to the wash-hand basin did not taste so bad.

'It's a little bit soapy,' Alice said, 'but perhaps that will boil out; like stains in table-cloths.'

It was a difficult question how to boil the pudding. Matilda proved furious when asked to let us, just because someone had happened to knock her hat off the scullery door and Pincher had got it and done for it. However, part of the embassy nicked a saucepan while the others were being told what Matilda thought about the hat, and we got hot water out of the bath-room and made it boil over our nursery fire. We put the pudding in – it was now getting on towards the hour of tea – and let it boil. With some exceptions – owing to the fine going down, and Matilda not hurrying up with coals – it boiled for an hour and a quarter. Then Matilda came suddenly in and said, 'I'm not going to have you messing about in here with my sauce-pans'; and she tried to take it off the fine. You will see that we couldn't stand this; it was not likely. I do not remember who it was that told her to mind her own business, and I think I have forgotten who caught hold of her first to make her chuck it. I am sure no needless violence was used. Anyway, while the struggle progressed, Alice and Dora took the saucepan away and put it in the boot-cupboard under the stairs and put the key in their pocket.

This sharp encounter made every one very hot and cross. We got over it before Matilda did, but we brought her round before bedtime. Quarrels should always be made up before bedtime. It says so in the Bible. If this simple rule was followed there would not be so many wars and martyrs and law suits and inquisitions and bloody deaths at the stake.

All the house was still. The gas was out all over the house except on the first landing, when several darkly shrouded figures might have been observed creeping downstairs to the kitchen.

On the way, with superior precaution, we got out our saucepan. The kitchen fire was red, but low; the coal-cellar was locked, and there was nothing in the scuttle but a little coal-dust and the piece of brown paper that is put in to keep the coals from tumbling out through the bottom where the hole is. We put the saucepan on the fire and plied it with fuel – two *Chronicles*, a *Telegraph*, and two *Family Herald* novelettes were burned in vain. I am almost sure the pudding did not boil at all that night.

'Never mind,' Alice said. 'We can each nick a piece of coal every time we go into the kitchen tomorrow.'

This daring scheme was faithfully performed, and by night we had nearly half a waste-paper basket of coal, coke, and cinders. And in the depth of night once more we might have been observed, this time with our collier-like waste-paper basket in our guarded hands.

There was more fire left in the grate that night, and we fed it with the fuel we had collected. This time the fire blazed up, and the pudding boiled like mad. This was the time it boiled two hours – at least I think it was about that, but we dropped asleep on the kitchen tables and dresser. You dare not be lowly in the night in the kitchen, because of the beetles. We were aroused by a horrible smell. It was the pudding-cloth burning. All the water had secretly boiled itself away. We filled it up at once with cold, and the saucepan cracked. So we cleaned it and put it back on the shelf and took another and went to bed. You see what a lot of trouble we had over the pudding. Every evening till Christmas, which had now become only the day after tomorrow, we sneaked down in the inky midnight and boiled that pudding for as long as it would.

On Christmas morning we chopped the holly for the sauce, but we put hot water (instead of brandy) and moist sugar. Some of them said it was not so bad. Oswald was not one of these.

Then came the moment when the plain pudding Father had ordered smoked upon the board. Matilda brought it in and went away at once. She had a cousin out of Woolwich Arsenal to see her that day, I remember. Those far-off days are quite distinct in memory's recollection still.

Then we got out our own pudding from its hiding-place and gave it one last hurried boil – only seven minutes, because of the general impatience which Oswald and Dora could not cope with.

We had found means to secrete a dish, and we now tried to dish the pudding up, but it stuck to the basin, and had to be dislodged with the chisel. The pudding was horribly pale. We poured the holly sauce over it, and Dora took up the knife and was just cutting it when a few simple words from H.O. turned us from happy and triumphing cookery artists to persons in despair.

He said: 'How pleased all those kind ladies and gentlemen would be if they knew *we* were the poor children they gave the shillings and sixpences and things for!'

We all said, '*What?*' It was no moment for politeness.

'I say,' H.O. said, 'they'd be glad if they knew it was us was enjoying the pudding, and not dirty little, really poor children.'

'You should say "you were", not "you was"', said Dora, but it was as in a dream and only from habit.

'Do you mean to say' – Oswald spoke firmly, yet not angrily – 'that you and Alice went and begged for money for poor children, and then *kept* it?'

'We didn't keep it,' said H.O., 'we spent it.'

'We've kept the *things*, you little duffer!' said Dicky, looking at the pudding sitting alone and uncared for on its dish. 'You begged for money for poor children, and then *kept* it. It's stealing, that's what it is. I don't say so much about you – you're only a silly kid – but Alice knew better. Why did you do it?'

He turned to Alice, but she was now too deep in tears to get a word out.

H.O. looked a bit frightened, but he answered the question. We have taught him this. He said –

'I thought they'd give us more if I said poor children than if I said just us.'

'*That's* cheating,' said Dicky, 'downright beastly, mean, low cheating.'

'I'm not,' said H.O.; 'and you're another.' Then he began to cry too. I do not know how the others felt, but I understand from Oswald that he felt that now the honour of the house of Bastable had been stamped on in the dust, and it didn't matter what happened. He looked at the beastly holly that had been left over from the sauce and was stuck up over the pictures. It now appeared hollow and disgusting, though it had got quite a lot of berries, and some of it was the varied kind – green and white. The figs and dates and toffee were set out in the doll's dinner service. The very sight of it all made Oswald blush sickly. He owns he would have liked to cuff H.O., and, if he did for a moment wish to shake Alice, the author, for one, can make allowances.

Now Alice choked and spluttered, and wiped her eyes fiercely, and said, 'It's no use ragging H.O. It's my fault. I'm older than he is.'

H.O. said, 'It couldn't be Alice's fault. I don't see as it was wrong.'

'That, not as,' murmured Dora, putting her arm round the sinner who had brought this degrading blight upon our family tree, but such is girls' undetermined and affectionate silliness. 'Tell sister all about it, H.O. dear. Why couldn't it be Alice's fault?'

H.O. cuddled up to Dora and said snufflingly in his nose –

'Because she hadn't got nothing to do with it. I collected it all. She never went into one of the houses. She didn't want to.'

'And then took all the credit of getting the money,' said Dicky savagely.

Oswald said, 'Not much *credit*,' in scornful tones.

'Oh, you are *beastly*, the whole lot of you, except Dora!' Alice said, stamping her foot in rage and despair. 'I tore my frock on a nail going out, and I didn't want to go back, and I got H.O. to go to the houses alone, and I waited for him outside. And I asked him not to say anything because

I didn't want Dora to know about the frock – it's my best. And I don't know what he said inside. He never told me. But I'll bet anything he didn't *mean* to cheat.'

'You *said* lots of kind people would be ready to give money to get pudding for poor children. So I asked them to.'

Oswald, with his strong right hand, waved a wave of passing things over.

'We'll talk about that another time,' he said; 'just now we've got weightier things to deal with.'

He pointed to the pudding, which had grown cold during the conversation to which I have alluded. H.O. stopped crying, but Alice went on with it. Oswald now said –

'We're a base and outcast family. Until that pudding's out of the house we shan't be able to look any one in the face. We must see that that pudding goes to poor children – not grisling, grumpy, whiney-piney, pretending poor children – but real poor ones, just as poor as they can stick.'

'And the figs too – and the dates,' said Noël, with regretting tones.

'Every fig,' said Dicky sternly. 'Oswald is quite right.'

This honourable resolution made us feel a bit better. We hastily put on our best things, and washed ourselves a bit, and hurried out to find some really poor people to give the pudding to. We cut it in slices ready, and put it in a basket with the figs and dates and toffee. We would not let H.O. come with us at first because he wanted to.

And Alice would not come because of him. So at last we had to let him. The excitement of tearing into your best things heals the hurt that wounded honour feels, as the poetry writer said – or at any rate it makes the hurt feel better.

We went out into the streets. They were pretty quiet – nearly everybody was eating its Christmas dessert. But presently we met a woman in an apron. Oswald said very politely –

'Please, are you a poor person?' And she told us to get along with us.

The next we met was a shabby man with a hole in his left boot.

Again Oswald said, 'Please, are you a poor person, and have you any poor little children?'

The man told us not to come any of our games with him, or we should laugh on the wrong side of our faces. We went on sadly. We had no heart to stop and explain to him that we had no games to come.

The next was a young man near the Obelisk. Dora tried this time.

She said, 'Oh, if you please we've got some Christmas pudding in this basket, and if you're a poor person you can have some.'

'Poor as Job,' said the young man in a hoarse voice, and he had to come up out of a red comforter to say it.

We gave him a slice of the pudding, and he bit into it without thanks or delay. The next minute he had thrown the pudding slap in Dora's face, and was clutching Dicky by the collar.

'Blime if I don't chuck ye in the river, the whole bloomin' lot of you!' he exclaimed.

The girls screamed, the boys shouted, and though Oswald threw himself on the insulter of his sister with all his manly vigour, yet but for a friend of Oswald's, who is in the police, passing at that instant, the author shudders to think what might have happened, for he was a strong young man, and Oswald is not yet come to his full strength, and the Quaggy runs all too near.

Our policeman led our assailant aside, and we waited anxiously, as he told us to. After long uncertain moments the young man in the comforter loafed off grumbling, and our policeman turned to us.

'Said you give him a dollop o' pudding, and it tasted of soap and hair-oil.'

I suppose the hair-oil must have been the Brown Windsoriness of the soap coming out. We were sorry, but it was still our duty to get rid of the pudding. The Quaggy was handy, it is true, but when you have collected money to feed poor children and spent it on pudding it is not right to throw that pudding in the river. People do not subscribe shillings and sixpences and half-crowns to feed a hungry flood with Christmas pudding.

Yet we shrank from asking any more people whether they were poor persons, or about their families, and still more from offering the pudding to chance people who might bite into it and taste the soap before we had time to get away.

It was Alice, the most paralysed with disgrace of all of us, who thought of the best idea.

She said, 'Let's take it to the workhouse. At any rate they're all poor people there, and they mayn't go out without leave, so they can't run after us to do anything to us after the pudding. No one would give them leave to go out to pursue people who had brought them pudding, and wreck vengeance on them, and at any rate we shall get rid of the conscience-pudding – it's a sort of conscience-money, you know – only it isn't money but pudding.'

The workhouse is a good way, but we stuck to it, though very cold, and hungrier than we thought possible when we started, for we had been so agitated we had not even stayed to eat the plain pudding our good Father had so kindly and thoughtfully ordered for our Christmas dinner.

The big bell at the workhouse made a man open the door to us, when we rang it. Oswald said (and he spoke because he is next eldest to Dora, and she had had jolly well enough of saying anything about pudding) – he said –

'Please we've brought some pudding for the poor people.'

He looked us up and down, and he looked at our basket, then he said: 'You'd better see the Matron.'

We waited in a hall, feeling more and more uncomfy, and less and less like Christmas. We were very cold indeed, especially our hands and our noses. And we felt less and less able to face the Matron if she was horrid, and one of us at least wished we had chosen the Quaggy for the pudding's long home, and made it up to the robbed poor in some other way afterwards.

Just as Alice was saying earnestly in the burning cold ear of Oswald, 'Let's put down the basket and make a bolt for it. Oh, Oswald, *let's*!' a lady came along the passage. She was very upright, and she had eyes that went through you like blue gimlets. I should not like to be obliged to thwart that lady if she had any design, and mine was opposite. I am glad this is not likely to occur.

She said, 'What's all this about a pudding?'

H.O. said at once, before we could stop him, 'They say I've stolen the pudding, so we've brought it here for the poor people.'

'No, we didn't!' 'That wasn't why!' 'The money was given!' 'It was meant for the poor!' 'Shut up, H.O.!' said the rest of us all at once.

Then there was an awful silence. The lady gimleted us again one by one with her blue eyes.

Then she said: 'Come into my room. You all look frozen.'

She took us into a very jolly room with velvet curtains and a big fire, and the gas lighted, because now it was almost dark, even out of doors. She gave us chairs, and Oswald felt as if his was a dock, he felt so criminal, and the lady looked so Judgular.

Then she took the arm-chair by the fire herself, and said, 'Who's the eldest?'

'I am,' said Dora, looking more like a frightened white rabbit than I've ever seen her.

'Then tell me all about it.'

Dora looked at Alice and began to cry. That slab of pudding in the face had totally unnerved the gentle girl. Alice's eyes were red, and her face was puffy with crying; but she spoke up for Dora and said –

'Oh, please let Oswald tell. Dora can't. She's tired with the long walk. And a young man threw a piece of it in her face, and –'

The lady nodded and Oswald began. He told the story from the very beginning, as he has always been taught to, though he hated to lay bare the family honour's wound before a stranger, however judgelike and gimlet-eyed. He told all – not concealing the pudding-throwing, nor what the young man said about soap.

'So,' he ended, 'we want to give the conscience-pudding to you. It's like conscience-money – you know what that is, don't you? But if you really think it is soapy and not just the young man's horridness, perhaps you'd better not let them eat it. But the figs and things are all right.'

When he had done the lady said, for most of us were crying more or less –

'Come, cheer up! It's Christmas-time, and he's very little – your brother, I mean. And I think the rest of you seem pretty well able to take care of the honour of the family. I'll take the conscience-pudding off your minds. Where are you going now?'

'Home, I suppose,' Oswald said. And he thought how nasty and dark and dull it would be. The fire out most likely and Father away.

'And your Father's not at home, you say,' the blue-gimlet lady went on. 'What do you say to having tea with me, and then seeing the entertainment we have got up for our old people?'

Then the lady smiled and the blue gimlets looked quite merry.

The room was so warm and comfortable and the invitation was the last thing we expected. It was jolly of her, I do think.

No one thought quite at first of saying how pleased we should be to accept her kind invitation. Instead we all just said 'Oh!' but in a tone which must have told her we meant 'Yes, please,' very deeply.

Oswald (this has more than once happened) was the first to restore his manners. He made a proper bow like he has been taught, and said –

'Thank you very much. We should like it very much. It is very much nicer than going home. Thank you very much.'

I need not tell the reader that Oswald could have made up a much better speech if he had had more time to make it up in, or if he had not been so filled with mixed flustered-ness and furification by the shameful events of the day.

We washed our faces and hands and had a first-rate muffin and crumpet tea, with slices of cold meats, and many nice jams and cakes. A lot of other people were there, most of them people who were giving the entertainment to the aged poor.

After tea it was the entertainment. Songs and conjuring and a play called 'Box and Cox', very amusing, and a lot of throwing things about in it – bacon and chops and things – and minstrels. We clapped till our hands were sore.

When it was over we said goodbye. In between the songs and things Oswald had had time to make up a speech of thanks to the lady.

He said –

'We all thank you heartily for your goodness. The entertainment was beautiful. We shall never forget your kindness and hospitableness.'

The lady laughed, and said she had been very pleased to have us. A fat gentleman said –

'And your teas? I hope you enjoyed those – eh?'

Oswald had not had time to make up an answer to that, so he answered straight from the heart, and said –

'Ra – *ther!*'

And everyone laughed and slapped us boys on the back and kissed the girls, and the gentleman who played the bones in the minstrels saw us home. We ate the cold pudding that night, and H.O. dreamed that something came to eat him, like it advises you to in the advertisements on the hoardings. The grown-ups said it was the pudding, but

I don't think it could have been that, because, as I have said more than once, it was so very plain.

Some of H.O.'s brothers and sisters thought it was a judgment on him for pretending about who the poor children were he was collecting the money for. Oswald does not believe such a little boy as H.O. would have a real judgment made just for him and nobody else, whatever he did.

But it certainly is odd. H.O. was the only one who had bad dreams, and he was also the only one who got any of the things we bought with that ill-gotten money, because, you remember, he picked a hole in the raisin-paper as he was bringing the parcel home. The rest of us had nothing, unless you count the scrapings of the pudding-basin, and those don't really count at all.

'Christmas at Cold Comfort Farm'
by Stella Gibbons

Stella Gibbons was born in London in 1902. She went to the North London Collegiate School and studied journalism at University College, London. She then worked for ten years on various papers, including the *Evening Standard*. Stella Gibbons is the author of twenty-five novels, three volumes of short stories, and four volumes of poetry. Her first publication was a book of poems, *The Mountain Beast* (1930), and her first novel, *Cold Comfort Farm* (1932), won the Femina Vie Heuruse Prize for 1933. Amongst her works are *Christmas at Cold Comfort Farm* (1940), *Westwood* (1946), *Conference at Cold Comfort Farm* (1959) and *Starlight* (1967). She was elected a Fellow of the Royal Society of Literature in 1950. In 1933 she married the actor and singer Allan Webb. They had one daughter. Stella Gibbons died in 1989.

Read more by Stella Gibbons:

Cold Comfort Farm

Starlight

Westwood

It was Christmas Eve. Dusk, a filthy mantle, lay over Sussex when the Reverend Silas Hearsay, Vicar of Howling, set out to pay his yearly visit to Cold Comfort Farm. Earlier in the afternoon he had feared he would not be Guided to go there, but then he had seen a crate of British Port-type wine go past the Vicarage on the grocer's boy's bicycle, and it could only be going, by that road, to the farmhouse. Shortly afterwards he was Guided to go, and set out upon his bicycle.

The Starkadders, of Cold Comfort Farm, had never got the hang of Christmas, somehow, and on Boxing Day there was always a run on the Howling Pharmacy for lint, bandages, and boracic powder. So the Vicar was going up there, as he did every year, to show them the ropes a bit. (It must be explained that these events took place some years before the civilising hand of Flora Poste had softened and reformed the Farm and its rude inhabitants.)

After removing two large heaps of tussocks which blocked the lane leading to the Farm and thereby releasing a flood of muddy, icy water over his ankles, the Vicar wheeled his machine on towards the farmhouse, reflecting that those tussocks had never fallen there from the dung-cart of Nature. It was clear that someone did not want him to come to the place. He pushed his bicycle savagely up the hill, muttering.

The farmhouse was in silence and darkness. He pulled the ancient hell-bell (once used to warn excommunicated persons to stay away from Divine Service) hanging outside the front door, and waited.

For a goodish bit nothing happened. Suddenly a window far above his head was flung open and a voice wailed into the twilight –

'No! No! No!'

And the window slammed shut again.

'You're making a mistake, I'm sure,' shouted the Vicar, peering up into the webby thongs of the darkness. 'It's me. The Rev Silas Hearsay.'

There was a pause. Then –

'Beant you postman?' asked the voice, rather embarrassed.

'No, no, of course not; come, come!' laughed the Vicar, grinding his teeth.

'I be comin',' retorted the voice. 'Thought it were postman after his Christmas Box.' The window slammed again. After a very long time indeed the door suddenly opened and there stood Adam Lambsbreath, oldest of the farm servants, peering up at the Reverend Hearsay by the light of a lonely rushdip (so called because you dipped it in grease and rushed to wherever you were going before it went out).

'Is anyone at home? May I enter?' enquired the Vicar, entering, and staring scornfully round the desolate kitchen, at the dead blue ashes in the grate, the thick dust on hanch and beam, the feathers blowing about like fun everywhere. Yet even here there were signs of Christmas, for a withered branch of holly stood in a shapeless vessel on the table. And Adam himself . . . there was something even more peculiar than usual about him.

'Are you ailing, man?' asked the Vicar irritably, kicking a chair out of the way and perching himself on the edge of the table.

'Nay, Rev, I be niver better,' piped the old man. '*The older the berry, The more it makes merry.*'

'Then why,' thundered the Vicar, sliding off the table and walking on tiptoe towards Adam with his arms held at full length above his head, 'are you wearing three of Mrs Starkadder's red shawls?'

Adam stood his ground.

'I mun have a red courtepy, master. Can't be Santa Claus wi'out a red courtepy,' he said. 'Iverybody knows that. Ay, the hand o' Fate lies heavy on us all, Christmas and all the year round alike, but I thought I'd bedight meself as Santa Claus, so I did, just to please me little Elfine. And this night at midnight I be goin' around fillin' the stockin's, if I'm spared.'

The Vicar laughed contemptuously.

'So that were why I took three o' Mrs Starkadder's red shawls,' concluded Adam.

'I suppose you have never thought of God in terms of Energy? No, it is too much to expect.' The Reverend Hearsay re-seated himself on the table and glanced at his watch. 'Where in Energy's name *is* everybody? I have to be at the Assembly Rooms to read a paper on *The Future of the Father Fixation* at eight, and I've got to feed first. If nobody's coming, I'd rather go.'

'Won't ee have a dram o' swede wine first?' a deep voice asked, and a tall woman stepped over the threshold, followed by a little girl of twelve or so with yellow hair and clear, beautiful features. Judith Starkadder dropped her hat on the floor and leant against the table, staring listlessly at the Vicar.

'No swede wine, I thank you,' snapped the Reverend Hearsay. He glanced keenly round the kitchen in search of the British Port-type, but there was no sign of it. 'I came up to discuss an article with you and yours. An article in *Home Anthropology.*'

''Twere good of ee, Reverend,' she said tiredly.

'It is called *Christmas: From Religious Festival to Shopping Orgy.* Puts the case for Peace and Good Will very sensibly. Both good for trade. What more can you want?'

'Nothing,' she said, leaning her head on her hand.

'But I see,' the Vicar went on furiously, in a low tone and glaring at Adam, 'that here, as everywhere else, the usual childish wish-fantasies are in possession. Stars,

shepherds, mangers, stockings, fir-trees, puddings . . .
Energy help you all! I wish you good night, and a
prosperous Christmas.'

He stamped out of the kitchen, and slammed the door
after him with such violence that he brought a slate down
on his back tyre and cut it open, and he had to walk home,
arriving there too late for supper before setting out for
Godmere.

After he had gone, Judith stared into the fire without
speaking, and Adam busied himself with scraping the
mould from a jar of mincemeat and picking some things
which had fallen into it out of a large crock of pudding
which he had made yesterday.

Elfine, meanwhile, was slowly opening a small
brown paper parcel which she had been nursing, and at
last revealed a small and mean-looking doll dressed in
a sleazy silk dress and one under-garment that did not
take off. This she gently nursed, talking to it in a low,
sweet voice.

'Who gave you that, child?' asked her mother idly.

'I told you, Mother. Uncle Micah and Aunt Rennett and
Aunt Prue and Uncle Harkaway and Uncle Ezra.'

'Treasure it. You will not get many such.'

'I know, Mother; I do. I love her very much, dear, dear
Caroline,' and Elfine gently put a kiss on the doll's face.

'Now, missus, have ee got the Year's Luck? Can't make
puddens wi'out the Year's Luck,' said Adam, shuffling
forward.

'It's somewhere here. I forget –'

She turned her shabby handbag upside down, and there fell out on the table the following objects:

A small coffin-nail.

A menthol cone.

Three bad sixpences.

A doll's cracked looking-glass.

A small roll of sticking-plaster.

Adam collected these objects and ranged them by the pudding basin.

'Ay, them's all there,' he muttered. 'Him as gets the sticking-plaster'll break a limb; the menthol cone means as you'll be blind wi' headache, the bad coins means as you'll lose all yer money, and him as gets the coffin-nail will die afore the New Year. The mirror's seven years' bad luck for someone. Aie! In ye go, curse ye!' and he tossed the objects into the pudding, where they were not easily nor long distinguishable from the main mass.

'Want a stir, missus? Come, Elfine, my popelot, stir long, stir firm, your meat to earn,' and he handed her the butt of an old rifle, once used by Fig Starkadder in the Gordon Riots.

Judith turned from the pudding with what is commonly described as a gesture of loathing, but Elfine took the rifle butt and stirred the mixture once or twice.

'Ay, now tes all mixed,' said the old man, nodding with satisfaction. 'Termorrer we'll boil un fer a good hour, and un'll be done.'

'Will an hour be enough?' said Elfine. 'Mrs Hawk-Monitor up at Hautcouture Hall boils hers for eight hours, and another four on Christmas Day.'

'How do ee know?' demanded Adam. 'Have ee been runnin' wi' that young goosepick Mus' Richard again?'

'You shut up. He's awfully decent.'

''Tisn't decent to run wi' a young popelot all over the Downs in all weathers.'

'Well, it isn't any of your business, so shut up.'

After an offended pause, Adam said:

'Well, niver fret about puddens. None of 'em here has iver tasted any puddens but mine, and they won't know no different.'

At midnight, when the farmhouse was in darkness save for the faint flame of a nightlight burning steadily beside the bed of Harkaway, who was afraid of bears, a dim shape might have been seen moving stealthily along the corridor from bedroom to bedroom. It wore three red shawls pinned over its torn nightshirt and carried over its shoulder a nose-bag (the property of Viper the gelding), distended with parcels. It was Adam, bent on putting into the stockings of the Starkadders the presents which he had made or bought with his savings. The presents were chiefly swedes, beet-roots, mangel-wurzels and turnips, decorated with coloured ribbons and strips of silver paper from tea packets.

'Ay,' muttered the old man, as he opened the door of the room where Meriam, the hired girl, was sleeping over the Christmas week. 'An apple for each will make 'em retch, a couple o' nuts will warm their wits.'

The next instant he stepped back in astonishment. There was a light in the room and there, sitting bolt upright in bed beside her slumbering daughter, was Mrs Beetle.

Mrs Beetle looked steadily at Adam, for a minute or two. Then she observed:

'Some 'opes.'

'Nay, niver say that, soul,' protested Adam, moving to the bedrail where hung a very fully fashioned salmon-pink silk stocking with ladders all down it. ''Tisn't so. Ee do know well that I looks on the maidy as me own child.'

Mrs Beetle gave a short laugh and adjusted a curler. 'You better not let Agony 'ear you, 'intin' I dunno wot,' said Mrs Beetle. ''Urry up and put yer rubbish in there, I want me sleep out; I got to be up at cock-wake termorrer.'

Adam put a swede, an apple and a small pot in the stocking and was tip-toeing away when Mrs Beetle, raising her head from the pillow, inquired:

'Wot's that you've give 'er?'

'Eye-shadow,' whispered Adam hoarsely, turning at the door.

'*Wot?*' hissed Mrs Beetle, inclining her head in an effort to hear. ''Ave you gorn crackers?'

'Eye-shadow. To put on the maidy's eyes. 'Twill give that touch o' glamour as be irresistible; it do say so on pot.'

'Get out of 'ere, you old trouble-maker! Don't she 'ave enough bother resistin' as it is, and then you go and give 'er . . . 'ere, wait till I –' and Mrs Beetle was looking around for something to throw as Adam hastily retreated.

'And I'll lay you ain't got no present fer me, ter make matters worse,' she called after him.

Silently he placed a bright new tin of beetle-killer on the washstand and shuffled away.

His experiences in the apartments of the other Stark-adders were no more fortunate, for Seth was busy with a friend and was so furious at being interrupted that he threw his riding-boots at the old man, Luke and Mark had locked their door and could be heard inside roaring with laughter at Adam's discomfiture, and Amos was praying, and did not even get up off his knees or open his eyes as he discharged at Adam the goat-pistol which he kept ever by his bed. And everybody else had such enormous holes in their stockings that the small presents Adam put in them fell through on to the floor along with the big ones, and when the Starkadders got up in the morning and rushed round to the foot of the bed to see what Santa had brought, they stubbed their toes on the turnips and swedes and walked on the smaller presents and smashed them to smithereens.

So what with one thing and another everybody was in an even worse temper than usual when the family assembled round the long table in the kitchen for the Christmas dinner about half-past two the next afternoon.

They would all have sooner been in some place else, but Mrs Ada Doom (Grandmother Doom, known as Grummer) insisted on them all being there, and as they did not want her to go mad and bring disgrace on the House of Starkadder, there they had to be.

One by one they came in, the men from the fields with soil on their boots, the women fresh from hennery and duck filch with eggs in their bosoms that they gave to Mrs Beetle who was just making the custard. Everybody had to work as usual on Christmas Day, and no one had troubled to put on anything handsomer than their usual workaday clouts stained with mud and plough-oil. Only Elfine wore a cherry-red jersey over her dark skirt and had pinned a spray of holly on herself. An aunt, a distant aunt named Mrs Poste, who lived in London, had unexpectedly sent her the pretty jersey. Prue and Letty had stuck sixpenny artificial posies in their hair, but they only looked wild and queer.

At last all were seated and waiting for Ada Doom.

'Come, come, mun we stick here like jennets i' the trave?' demanded Micah at last. 'Amos, Reuben, do ee carve the turkey. If so be as we wait much longer, 'twill be shent, and the sausages, too.'

Even as he spoke, heavy footsteps were heard approaching the head of the stairs, and everybody at once rose to their feet and looked towards the door.

The low-ceilinged room was already half in dusk, for it was a cold, still Christmas Day, without much light in the grey sky, and the only other illumination came from the dull fire, half-buried under a tass of damp kindling.

Adam gave a last touch to the pile of presents, wrapped in hay and tied with bast, which he had put round the foot of the withered thorn-branch that was the traditional Starkadder Christmas-tree, hastily rearranged one of the tufts of sheep's-wool that decorated its branches, straightened the raven's skeleton that adorned its highest branch in place of a fairy-doll or star, and shuffled into his place just as Mrs Doom reached the foot of the stairs, leaning on her daughter Judith's arm. Mrs Doom struck at him with her stick in passing as she went slowly to the head of the table.

'Well, well. What are we waiting for? Are you all mishooden?' she demanded impatiently as she seated herself. 'Are you all here? All? Answer me!' banging her stick.

'Ay, Grummer,' rose the low, dreary drone from all sides of the table. 'We be all here.'

'Where's Seth?' demanded the old woman, peering sharply on either side of the long row.

'Gone out,' said Harkaway briefly, shifting a straw in his mouth.

'What for?' demanded Mrs Doom.

There was an ominous silence.

'He said he was going to fetch something, Grandmother,' at last said Elfine.

'Ay. Well, well, no matter, so long as he comes soon.

Amos, carve the bird. Ay, would it were a vulture, 'twere more fitting! Reuben, fling these dogs the fare my bounty provides. Sausages . . . pah! Mince-pies . . . what a black-bitter mockery it all is! Every almond, every raisin, is wrung from the dry, dying soil and paid for with sparse greasy notes grudged alike by bank and buyer. Come, Ezra, pass the ginger wine! Be gay, spawn! Laugh, stuff your-selves, gorge and forget, you rat-heaps! Rot you all!' and she fell back in her chair, gasping and keeping one eye on the British Port-type that was now coming up the table.

'Tes one of her bad days,' said Judith tonelessly. 'Amos, will you pull a cracker wi' me? We were lovers . . . once.'

'Hush, woman.' He shrank back from the proffered treat. 'Tempt me not wi' motters and paper caps. Hell is paved wi' such.' Judith smiled bitterly and fell silent.

Reuben, meanwhile, had seen to it that Elfine got the best bit off the turkey (which is not saying much) and had filled her glass with Port-type wine and well-water.

The turkey gave out before it got to Letty, Prue, Susan, Phoebe, Jane and Rennett, who were huddled together at the foot of the table, and they were making do with Brussels sprouts as hard as bullets drenched with weak gravy, and home-brewed braket. There was silence in the kitchen except for the sough of swallowing, the sudden suck of drinking.

'WHERE IS SETH?' suddenly screamed Mrs Doom, flinging down her turkey-leg and glaring round.

Silence fell; everyone moved uneasily, not daring to

speak in case they provoked an outburst. But at that moment the cheerful, if unpleasant, noise of a motor-cycle was heard outside, and in another moment it stopped at the kitchen door. All eyes were turned in that direction, and in another moment in came Seth.

'Well, Grummer! Happen you thought I was lost!' he cried impudently, peeling off his boots and flinging them at Meriam, the hired girl, who cowered by the fire gnawing a sausage skin.

Mrs Doom silently pointed to his empty seat with the turkey-leg, and he sat down.

'She hev had an outhees. Ay, 'twas terrible,' reproved Judith in a low tone as Seth seated himself beside her.

'Niver mind, I ha' something here as will make her chirk like a mellet,' he retorted, and held up a large brown paper parcel. 'I ha' been to the Post Office to get it.'

'Ah, gie it me! Aie, my lost pleasurings! Tes none I get, nowadays; gie it me now!' cried the old woman eagerly.

'Nay, Grummer. Ee must wait till pudden time,' and the young man fell on his turkey ravenously.

When everyone had finished, the women cleared away and poured the pudding into a large dusty dish, which they bore to the table and set before Judith.

'Amos? Pudding?' she asked listlessly. 'In a glass or on a plate?'

'On plate, on plate, woman,' he said feverishly bending forward with a fierce glitter in his eye. 'Tes easier to see the Year's Luck so.'

A stir of excitement now went through the company, for everybody looked forward to seeing everybody else drawing ill-luck from the symbols concealed in the pudding. A fierce, attentive silence fell. It was broken by a wail from Reuben –

'The coin – the coin! Wala wa!' and he broke into deep, heavy sobs. He was saving up to buy a tractor, and the coin meant, of course, that he would lose all his money during the year.

'Never mind, Reuben, dear,' whispered Elfine, slipping an arm round his neck. 'You can have the penny father gave me.'

Shrieks from Letty and Prue now announced that they had received the menthol cone and the sticking-plaster, and a low mutter of approval greeted the discovery by Amos of the broken mirror.

Now there was only the coffin-nail, and a ghoulish silence fell on everybody as they dripped pudding from their spoons in a feverish hunt for it; Ezra was running his through a tea-strainer.

But no one seemed to have got it.

'Who has the coffin-nail? Speak, you draf-saks!' at last demanded Mrs Doom.

'Not I.' 'Nay.' 'Niver sight nor snitch of it,' chorused everybody.

'Adam!' Mrs Doom turned to the old man. 'Did you put the coffin-nail into the pudding?'

'Ay, mistress, that I did – didn't I, Mis' Judith, didn't I, Elfine, my liddle lovesight?'

'He speaks truth for once, mother.'

'Yes, he did, Grandmother. I saw him.'

'*Then where is it?*' Mrs Doom's voice was low and terrible and her gaze moved slowly down the table, first on one side and then the other, in search of signs of guilt, while everyone cowered over their plates.

Everyone, that is, except Mrs Beetle, who continued to eat a sandwich that she had taken out of a cellophane wrapper, with every appearance of enjoyment.

'Carrie Beetle!' shouted Mrs Doom.

'I'm 'ere,' said Mrs Beetle.

'Did you take the coffin-nail out of the pudding?'

'Yes, I did.' Mrs Beetle leisurely finished the last crumb of sandwich and wiped her mouth with a clean handkerchief. 'And will again, if I'm spared till next year.'

'You . . . you . . . you . . .' choked Mrs Doom, rising in her chair and beating the air with her clenched fists. 'For two hundred years . . . Starkadders . . . coffin-nails in puddings . . . and now . . . you . . . dare . . .'

'Well, I 'ad enough of it las' year,' retorted Mrs Beetle. 'That pore old soul Earnest Dolour got it, as well you may remember –'

'That's right. Cousin Earnest,' nodded Mark Dolour. 'Got a job workin' on the oil-field down Henfield way. Good money, too.'

'Thanks to me, if he 'as,' retorted Mrs Beetle. 'If I 'adn't put it up to you, Mark Dolour, you'd 'ave let 'im die. All of you was 'angin' over the pore old soul waitin' for 'im to 'and in 'is dinner pail, and Micah (wot's old enough to know better, 'eaven only knows) askin' 'im could 'e 'ave 'is wrist-watch if anything was to 'appen to 'im . . . it fair got me down. So I says to Mark, why don't yer go down and 'ave a word with Mr Earthdribble the undertaker in Howling and get 'im to tell Earnest it weren't a proper coffin-nail at all, it were a throw-out, so it didn't count. The bother we 'ad! Shall I ever fergit it! Never again, I says to meself. So this year there ain't no coffin-nail. I fished it out o' the pudden meself. Parss the water, please.'

'Where is it?' whispered Mrs Doom, terribly. 'Where is this year's nail, woman?'

'Down the –' Mrs Beetle checked herself, and coughed, 'down the well,' concluded Mrs Beetle firmly.

'Niver fret, Grummer, I'll get it up fer ee! Me and the water voles, we can dive far and deep!' and Urk rushed from the room, laughing wildly.

'There ain't no need,' called Mrs Beetle after him. 'But anything to keep you an' yer rubbishy water voles out of mischief!' And Mrs Beetle went into a cackle of laughter, alternately slapping her knee and Caraway's arm, and muttering, 'Oh, cor, wait till I tell Agony! "Dive far and deep." Oh, cor!' After a minute's uneasy silence –

'Grummer.' Seth bent winningly towards the old woman, the large brown paper parcel in his hand. 'Will you see your present now?'

'Aye, boy, aye. Let me see it. You're the only one that has thought of me, the only one.'

Seth was undoing the parcel, and now revealed a large book, handsomely bound in red leather with gilt lettering.

'There, Grummer. 'Tis the year's numbers o' *The Milk Producers' Weekly Bulletin and Cowkeepers' Guide*. I collected un for ee, and had un bound. Art pleased?'

'Ay. 'Tis handsome enough. A graceful thought,' muttered the old lady, turning the pages. Most of them were pretty battered, owing to her habit of rolling up the paper and hitting anyone with it who happened to be within reach. ''Tis better so. 'Tis heavier. Now I can *throw* it.'

The Starkadders so seldom saw a clean and handsome object at the farmhouse (for Seth was only handsome) that they now crept round, fascinated, to examine the book with murmurs of awe. Among them came Adam, but no sooner had he bent over the book than he recoiled from it with a piercing scream.

'Aie! . . . aie! aie!'

'What's the matter, dotard?' screamed Mrs Doom, jabbing at him with the volume. 'Speak, you kaynard!'

'Tes calf! Tes bound in calf! And tes our Pointless's calf, as she had last Lammastide, as was sold at Godmere to Farmer Lust!' cried Adam, falling to the floor. At the same instant, Luke hit Micah in the stomach, Harkaway pushed Ezra into the fire, Mrs Doom flung the bound volume of *The Milk Producers' Weekly Bulletin and Cowkeepers' Guide* at the struggling mass, and the Christmas dinner collapsed into indescribable confusion.

In the midst of the uproar, Elfine, who had climbed on to the table, glanced up at the window as though seeking help, and saw a laughing face looking at her, and a hand in a yellow string glove beckoning with a riding-crop. Swiftly she darted down from the table and across the room, and out through the half-open door, slamming it after her.

Dick Hawk-Monitor, a sturdy boy astride a handsome pony, was out in the yard.

'Hallo!' she gasped. 'Oh, Dick, I am glad to see you!'

'I thought you never would see me – what on earth's the matter in there?' he asked curiously.

'Oh, never mind them, they're always like that. Dick, do tell me, what presents did you have?'

'Oh, a rifle, and a new saddle, and a fiver – lots of things. Look here, Elfine, you mustn't mind, but I brought you –' He bent over the pony's neck and held out a sandwich box, daintily filled with slices of turkey, a piece of pudding, a tiny mince-pie and a crystallised apricot.

'Thought your dinner mightn't be very –' he ended gruffly.

'Oh, Dick, it's lovely! Darling little . . . what is it?'

'Apricot. Crystallised fruit. Look here, let's go up to the usual place, shall we? – and I'll watch you eat it.'

'But you must have some, too.'

'Man! I'm stoked up to the brim now! But I dare say I could manage a bit more. Here, you catch hold of Rob Roy, and he'll help you up the hill.'

He touched the pony with his heels and it trotted on towards the snow-streaked Downs, Elfine's yellow hair flying out like a shower of primroses under the grey sky of winter.

'There Never Was Such a Goose' from
A Christmas Carol by Charles Dickens

Charles Dickens was born in Hampshire on 7 February 1812. His father was a clerk in the navy pay office, who was well paid but often ended up in financial troubles. His career as a writer of fiction started in 1833 when his short stories and essays began to appear in periodicals. *The Pickwick Papers*, his first commercial success, was published in 1836. *Oliver Twist* and many other novels followed. *The Old Curiosity Shop* brought Dickens international fame and he became a celebrity in America as well as in Britain. Charles Dickens died on 9 June 1870, leaving his last novel, *The Mystery of Edwin Drood*, unfinished. He is buried in Westminster Abbey.

In this extract from Dickens's short novel *A Christmas Carol*, the Ghost of Christmas Present has conducted the miser Scrooge to the home of his poor clerk, Bob Cratchit, where, invisible, they observe the Cratchit family's celebrations.

Read more by Charles Dickens:
A Christmas Carol
David Copperfield
Great Expectations

Then up rose Mrs Cratchit, Cratchit's wife, dressed out but poorly in a twice-turned gown, but brave in ribbons, which are cheap and make a goodly show for sixpence; and she laid the cloth, assisted by Belinda Cratchit, second of her daughters, also brave in ribbons; while Master Peter Cratchit plunged a fork into the saucepan of potatoes, and getting the corners of his monstrous shirt-collar (Bob's private property, conferred upon his son and heir in honour of the day) into his mouth, rejoiced to find himself so gallantly attired, and yearned to show his linen in the fashionable Parks. And now two smaller Cratchits, boy and girl, came tearing in, screaming that outside the baker's they had smelt the goose, and known it for their own; and basking in luxurious thoughts of sage and onion, these young Cratchits danced about the table, and exalted Master Peter Cratchit to the skies, while he (not proud, although his collars nearly choked him) blew the fire, until the slow potatoes bubbling up, knocked loudly at the saucepan-lid to be let out and peeled.

'What has ever got your precious father then,' said Mrs Cratchit. 'And your brother, Tiny Tim; and Martha warn't as late last Christmas Day by half-an-hour!'

'Here's Martha, mother!' said a girl, appearing as she spoke.

'Here's Martha, mother!' cried the two young Cratchits. 'Hurrah! There's *such* a goose, Martha!'

'Why, bless your heart alive, my dear, how late you are!' said Mrs Cratchit, kissing her a dozen times, and taking off her shawl and bonnet for her, with officious zeal.

'We'd a deal of work to finish up last night,' replied the girl, 'and had to clear away this morning, mother!'

'Well! Never mind so long as you are come,' said Mrs Cratchit. 'Sit ye down before the fire, my dear, and have a warm, Lord bless ye!'

'No no! There's Father coming,' cried the two young Cratchits, who were everywhere at once. 'Hide Martha, hide!'

So Martha hid herself, and in came little Bob, the father, with at least three feet of comforter exclusive of the fringe, hanging down before him; and his thread-bare clothes darned up and brushed, to look seasonable; and Tiny Tim upon his shoulder. Alas for Tiny Tim, he bore a little crutch, and had his limbs supported by an iron frame!

'Why, where's our Martha?' cried Bob Cratchit looking round.

'Not coming,' said Mrs Cratchit.

'Not coming!' said Bob, with a sudden declension in his high spirits; for he had been Tim's blood horse all the way from church, and had come home rampant. 'Not coming upon Christmas Day!'

Martha didn't like to see him disappointed, if it were only in joke; so she came out prematurely from behind the closet door, and ran into his arms, while the two young Cratchits hustled Tiny Tim, and bore him off into the wash-house, that he might hear the pudding singing in the copper.

'And how did little Tim behave?' asked Mrs Cratchit, when she had rallied Bob on his credulity and Bob had hugged his daughter to his heart's content.

'As good as gold,' said Bob, 'and better. Somehow he gets thoughtful sitting by himself so much, and thinks the strangest things you ever heard. He told me, coming home, that he hoped the people saw him in the church, because he was a cripple, and it might be pleasant to them to remember upon Christmas Day, who made lame beggars walk and blind men see.'

Bob's voice was tremulous when he told them this, and trembled more when he said that Tiny Tim was growing strong and hearty.

His active little crutch was heard upon the floor, and back came Tiny Tim before another word was spoken, escorted by his brother and sister to his stool before the fire; and while Bob, turning up his cuffs – as if, poor fellow, they were capable of being made more shabby – compounded some hot mixture in a jug with gin and lemons, and stirred it round and round and put it on the hob to simmer; Master Peter, and the two ubiquitous young Cratchits went to fetch the goose, with which they soon returned in high procession.

Such a bustle ensued that you might have thought a goose the rarest of all birds; a feathered phenomenon, to which a black swan was a matter of course; and in truth it was something very like it in that house. Mrs Cratchit made the gravy (ready beforehand in a little saucepan) hissing hot; Master Peter mashed the potatoes with incredible vigour; Miss Belinda sweetened up the apple-sauce; Martha dusted the hot plates; Bob took Tiny Tim beside him in a tiny corner at the table; the two young Cratchits set chairs for everybody, not forgetting themselves, and mounting guard upon their posts, crammed spoons into their mouths, lest they should shriek for goose before their turn came to be helped. At last the dishes were set on, and grace was said. It was succeeded by a breathless pause, as Mrs Cratchit, looking slowly all along the carving-knife, prepared to plunge it in the breast; but when she did, and when the long expected gush of stuffing issued forth, one murmur of delight arose all round the board, and even Tiny Tim, excited by the two young Cratchits, beat on the table with the handle of his knife, and feebly cried Hurrah!

There never was such a goose. Bob said he didn't believe there ever was such a goose cooked. Its tenderness and flavour, size and cheapness, were the themes of universal admiration. Eked out by the apple-sauce and mashed potatoes, it was a sufficient dinner for the whole family; indeed, as Mrs Cratchit said with great delight (surveying one small atom of a bone upon the dish), they hadn't ate it all at last! Yet every one had had enough, and the youngest Cratchits in particular, were steeped in sage and onion to the eyebrows! But now, the plates being changed by Miss Belinda, Mrs Cratchit left the room alone – too nervous to bear witnesses – to take the pudding up, and bring it in.

Suppose it should not be done enough! Suppose it should break in turning out! Suppose somebody should have got over the wall of the backyard, and stolen it, while they were merry with the goose: a supposition at which the two young Cratchits became livid! All sorts of horrors were supposed.

Hallo! A great deal of steam! The pudding was out of the copper. A smell like a washing-day! That was the cloth. A smell like an eating-house, and a pastry cook's next door to each other, with a laundress's next door to that! That was the pudding. In half a minute Mrs Cratchit entered: flushed, but smiling proudly: with the pudding, like a speckled cannon-ball, so hard and firm, blazing in half of half-a-quartern of ignited brandy, and bedight with Christmas holly stuck into the top.

Oh, a wonderful pudding! Bob Cratchit said, and calmly too, that he regarded it as the greatest success achieved by Mrs Cratchit since their marriage. Mrs Cratchit said that now the weight was off her mind, she would confess she had

had her doubts about the quantity of flour. Everybody had something to say about it, but nobody said or thought it was at all a small pudding for a large family. It would have been flat heresy to do so. Any Cratchit would have blushed to hint at such a thing.

At last the dinner was all done, the cloth was cleared, the hearth swept, and the fire made up. The compound in the jug being tasted, and considered perfect, apples and oranges were put upon the table, and a shovel-full of chestnuts on the fire. Then all the Cratchit family drew round the hearth, in what Bob Cratchit called a circle, meaning half a one; and at Bob Cratchit's elbow stood the family display of glass; two tumblers, and a custard-cup without a handle.

These held the hot stuff from the jug, however, as well as golden goblets would have done; and Bob served it out with beaming looks, while the chestnuts on the fire sputtered and crackled noisily. Then Bob proposed:

'A Merry Christmas to us all, my dears. God bless us!'

Which all the family re-echoed.

'God bless us every one!' said Tiny Tim, the last of all. He sat very close to his father's side, upon his little stool. Bob held his withered little hand in his, as if he loved the child, and wished to keep him by his side, and dreaded that he might be taken from him.

'Spirit,' said Scrooge, with an interest he had never felt before, 'tell me if Tiny Tim will live.'

'I see a vacant seat,' replied the Ghost, 'in the poor chimney corner, and a crutch without an owner, carefully preserved. If these shadows remain unaltered by the Future, the child will die.'

'No, no,' said Scrooge. 'Oh no, kind Spirit! say he will be spared.'

'If these shadows remain unaltered by the Future, none other of my race,' returned the Ghost, 'will find him here. What then? If he be like to die, he had better do it, and decrease the surplus population.'

Scrooge hung his head to hear his own words quoted by the Spirit, and was overcome with penitence and grief.

'Man,' said the Ghost, 'if man you be in heart, not adamant, forbear that wicked cant until you have discovered What the surplus is, and Where it is. Will you decide what men shall live, what men shall die? It may be, that in the sight of Heaven, you are more worthless and less fit to live than millions like this poor man's child. Oh God! to hear the Insect on the leaf pronouncing on the too much life among his hungry brothers in the dust!'

Scrooge bent before the Ghost's rebuke, and trembling cast his eyes upon the ground. But he raised them speedily, on hearing his own name.

'Mr Scrooge!' said Bob; 'I'll give you Mr Scrooge, the Founder of the Feast!'

'The Founder of the Feast indeed!' cried Mrs Cratchit, reddening. 'I wish I had him here. I'd give him a piece of my mind to feast upon, and I hope he'd have a good appetite for it.'

'My dear,' said Bob, 'the children; Christmas Day.'

'It should be Christmas Day, I am sure,' said she, 'on which one drinks the health of such an odious, stingy, hard, unfeeling man as Mr Scrooge. You know he is, Robert! Nobody knows it better than you do, poor fellow!'

'My dear,' was Bob's mild answer, 'Christmas Day.'

'I'll drink his health for your sake and the Day's,' said Mrs Cratchit, 'not for his. Long life to him! A merry Christmas and a happy new year! – he'll be very merry and very happy, I have no doubt!'

The children drank the toast after her. It was the first of their proceedings which had no heartiness in it. Tiny Tim drank it last of all, but he didn't care twopence for it. Scrooge was the Ogre of the family. The mention of his name cast a dark shadow on the party, which was not dispelled for full five minutes.

After it had passed away, they were ten times merrier than before, from the mere relief of Scrooge the Baleful being done with. Bob Cratchit told them how he had a situation in his eye for Master Peter, which would bring in, if obtained, full five-and-sixpence weekly. The two young Cratchits laughed tremendously at the idea of Peter's being a man of business; and Peter himself looked thoughtfully at the fire from between his collars, as if he were deliberating what particular investments he should favour when he came into the receipt of that bewildering income. Martha, who was a poor apprentice at a milliner's, then told them what kind of work she had to do, and how many hours she worked at a stretch, and how she meant to lie a-bed tomorrow morning for a good long rest; tomorrow being a holiday she passed at home. Also how she had seen a countess and a lord some days before, and how the lord 'was much about as tall as Peter'; at which Peter pulled up his collars so high that you couldn't have seen his head if you had been there. All this time the chestnuts and the jug went round and round; and bye and bye they had a song, about a lost child travelling in the snow, from Tiny Tim; who had a plaintive little voice, and sang it very well indeed.

There was nothing of high mark in this. They were not a handsome family; they were not well dressed; their shoes were far from being water-proof; their clothes were scanty; and Peter might have known, and very likely did, the inside of a pawn-broker's. But they were happy, grateful, pleased with one another, and contented with the time; and when they faded, and looked happier yet in the bright sprinklings of the Spirit's torch at parting, Scrooge had his eye upon them, and especially on Tiny Tim, until the last.

'Let Nothing You Dismay'
by Helen Simpson

Helen Simpson writes sharply funny, brilliantly observed short stories, and with each of her six collections, one published every five years since *Four Bare Legs in a Bed* in 1990, she has been hailed as a 'contemporary maestro of the short story' (*Sunday Times*). Before writing her first stories, Helen Simpson was a staff writer at *Vogue* and published two cookery books. She lives in London, and her latest collection is *Cockfosters* (2015).

Read more by Helen Simpson:

Dear George

Hey Yeah Right Get a Life

Constitutional

The tree was bigger than ever, eight feet tall, a bushy Douglas fir making the furniture round it look pathetically tame. Lametta icicles dangled from its needles, silver reflecting white from the snow outside, and little painted apples on ribbons. These apples transformed it into a medieval Paradise tree, absolved by Christ's birth from the curse laid upon it in the garden of Eden, though nobody in the house was aware of this, least of all fifteen-year-old Miranda Otway, who was lounging beneath its green boughs whispering sweet nothings down the telephone to Colin Smith.

A hard-faced boy came in, agitated the little snowscene of the man and woman standing in a forest, snapped off a sprig of mistletoe, and kissed Miranda, who covered the receiver and preserved a mouth of stone until he went away again. Then, 'Nothing,' she whispered. 'Just that creep Jasper I told you about that Daddy asked for Christmas.'

Over on the table by her father's armchair lay *The Pickwick Papers*, open at chapter twenty-eight in case any one should care to take up the flutter-leafed volume and read aloud in a plummy voice, as he, Tarquin Otway, paterfamilias, liked to do. The night before, on Christmas Eve, Tarquin had gathered them all round him to join in a rousing seasonal medley before supper, and there was his favourite volume of carols on top of the piano now, packed with opulent gallery-backed reproductions: a della Robbia virgin against blue-glazed heavens; Flemish magi; oak angels springing from carved choir stalls; seven satin-stitched swans a-swimming; a star sending golden streamers down to a gold-strawed crib.

'Do you know, the Deerhursts put a card through the door last night,' said Jane Otway, plucking her husband into the room by his shirtsleeve, pouncing on a glossy scene of gluttony above the fireplace. 'After we'd gone to bed. They are infuriating. They do it on purpose. They know we don't hit it off.'

'A cheap trick,' Tarquin agreed.

'I think Miranda has asked this new boyfriend to tea, by the way,' said Jane. 'So be warned.'

Miranda had meanwhile joined her five-year-old sister Susan in answering the door to their grandmother, and was now puzzling over twisted coatsleeve linings and spare cardigans.

'Happy Christmas, Mummy,' crowed Jane, coming into the hall. 'Happy Christmas.'

'If you say so,' said her mother, eyeing her narrowly. 'You're looking very fat, Jane. You're not pregnant again?'

'I can assure you she's not!' chuckled Tarquin, giving his mother-in-law a symbolic embrace, holding her for a moment as though she were a corn dolly or similarly fragile item of folk art. 'How are you, Cynthia?'

'Oh, you know,' she said, cross, flirtatious.

'A glass of ginger wine,' he announced in his glad ecclesiastical voice.

'I hate to think what's happening out there,' said Tarquin from the head of the table. 'She should have left it to me. I think I can safely claim to know more about geese than Jane does.'

'That wouldn't be difficult,' said Jane's mother, with a dry laugh.

'The inexperienced trying to cook the inappropriate,' said Tarquin. 'What was it Oscar said? The ignoramus, was it? The incoherent? Oh, something something something.'

Jasper chuckled sycophantically.

'Well, you'll be up at Oriel before we know it,' said Tarquin, turning to him fondly. 'You'll soon be able to put me right.'

'I can't eat this soup,' piped Susan. 'It's horrible.'

'*Soupe de poissons* from Marseille,' said Tarquin, 'is not horrible whatever else it is. I hope she's remembered to save the fat.'

'I can't eat the soup either,' said Miranda.

'Goose dripping sandwiches,' said Tarquin fondly. 'With a spot of vinegar. Oh, you. You can't eat anything. On principle.'

'Vegetarian!' said Jane's mother, and laughed.

'Vegetarian,' said Tarquin. 'Why can't you do something constructive. Like bell ringing. Gloria in excelsis. By the way, where's this friend of yours "Colin" destined for?'

Miranda shrugged and stared at her plate.

'Oriel,' said Jasper thoughtfully. 'Only if my results are all right, of course.'

'They will be,' said Tarquin. 'Chip off the old block. Your father and I up at Oriel together. Squash, rugger, rowing, whatever you care to mention. Nights in the bar. Now I'm in Hertfordshire and he's in Melbourne. Extraordinary! Here's to Charlie, anyway. And we're glad to have you with us today, Jasper, as you couldn't join your own family.'

'Oh, plum pudding on the beach,' said Jasper. 'Not really my scene.'

'Anyway,' said Tarquin, raising his glass. 'To the family.'

'I don't know how you can, Daddy,' said Miranda. 'Pretending to be all nicey nice at Christmas when you hardly ever see us the rest of the year.'

'Somebody's got to pay your school fees, my dear,' said Tarquin with a tight smile. 'Put this not insubstantial roof over our heads.'

Just then, Jane tottered into the room on a cloud of steam like the genie of the lamp. When she had put the goose into the oven, three hours ago, it had been a large oval-breasted cadaver. During the morning she had had to pour off several pints of the fat which she now realised had been its chief constituent. Much of this fat seemed to have made its way onto her clothes and hair and skin. The goose, meanwhile, had continued to melt like a candle, and was now rather less than half its former size. She placed it in front of Tarquin along with the carving implements.

'Another thing, Daddy,' Miranda was saying. 'We all heard you in church crackling that twenty-pound note before you put it on the plate. Talk about showing off.'

'Good will to all men,' said Tarquin pleasantly, shaving off fine-grained leaves of goose with expert relish. 'The time of year to think of those less fortunate than our-selves. Etcetera. You heard the vicar, Miranda.'

'Oh honestly,' said Miranda.

'Go on,' said Tarquin, tucking in. 'Tell me the homeless are all my fault. Beat me up with the cardboard boxes.'

'Twenty pounds,' said Miranda. 'It's an insult. You should give a tenth of your income. A third!'

'I already do, via the Inland Revenue. More!' said Tarquin. 'Now crush me with the single mothers.'

'The crib was a bit disappointing this year,' said Jane. 'Everybody thought so. The three kings were awfully drab. Anyway, Miranda, we've got a standing order with Save the Children.'

'Do you know what's happening in the world?' bellowed Miranda. 'Wars. Earthquakes. Torture. Then you pretend you believe in God.'

'I suppose this Colin is a lefty,' said Tarquin.

'Sometimes,' said Miranda, 'I really hate you.'

'Now, now, Tiny Tim,' said Tarquin. 'Or should it be Timette. Tiny Timette. Rather a good name for a large-boned girl like you. Should you choose to go in for prize wrestling.'

Jasper almost fell off his chair laughing.

Later that afternoon, Jane was preparing the tea.

'You will be nice to this Colin boy, darling?' she said to her husband, who was lolling against the kitchen dresser under a post-prandial cloud of alcohol.

'Some oversexed young yob brought home expressly to annoy me,' he grumbled, throwing a chunk of stollen into his mouth. 'To insult us.'

'You never know,' said Jane, fanning out a line of Dutch spice biscuits. 'He may be a very nice boy.'

And when at last Colin appeared, shifting from desert boot to desert boot on the doormat, it seemed that he was indeed exactly that. Tall, broad-shouldered, shy and beautiful, he was every inch the handsome prince. His long dark hair, spangled with six-cornered snowflakes, was tied back in a pony tail.

'Pleased to meet you,' he said, and with a horrified look watched himself wipe his hand on his trouser leg before offering it to Tarquin.

'Miranda will be down in a minute,' said Jane. 'Do come in.'

Colin loped over to the shelter of the sideboard, where he stood at bay, his eyes skittering over silver-coated almonds, muscatel raisins, and half a dozen Mandarin oranges, skinless, sodden, stacked in a crystal tower of Cointreau.

'We usually play a game or two before tea at Christmas,' said Tarquin. 'Do you like games, Colin?'

'What, er you mean, cards?' said Colin.

'Well, I was thinking more of Botticelli,' purred Tarquin. 'Charades. That sort of thing.'

'Dumb Crambo,' said Jasper.

'Right,' said Colin. 'Right.'

There was a bowl of pot-pourri at his elbow, snuffcoloured rose petals, parched and faded; he grabbed a nervous handful, imagining them to be some sort of posh crisps, and thrust it into his mouth.

Everyone stared, transfixed, as Colin chewed. Susan said, 'Can I have one?'

Miranda came into the room, and her eyes met his. He gave an heroic swallow and gasped her name. They smiled at each other uncontrollably.

'How many brothers and sisters have you got?' piped Susan.

'Two brothers, both older than me,' he said, ruffling her hair. 'No sisters.'

'Oh,' said Susan, and stood hugging his left leg and smiling up at him like a kitten.

'I hope your mother doesn't mind us stealing you like this on Christmas Day,' said Jane.

'No,' said Colin. 'Mum died. Nearly three years ago now.'

'Oh I am sorry,' said Jane.

'Yeah,' said Colin. 'But we're all right.'

'Was it … ?' said Tarquin.

'Cancer,' said Colin.

'What, er, what sort?' asked Tarquin.

'Oh. Er. Lung cancer,' said Colin, lifting his chin.

'Ah.' Tarquin paused. 'She was a smoker, then?'

'Daddy!' said Miranda.

'Three years,' said Tarquin. 'Pretty much back to normal, I expect, now that the, er, dust has settled?'

'Not very cheerful at Christmas, though,' said Jane.

'It's not been that bad,' said Colin. 'My friend at school, now, he's had a bad Christmas all right. His mother ran off with her boyfriend in November, and his father, he's a drinker, he chucked him out last night. Nowhere to go. No money. He's dossing down with us for a few nights but my dad says he's got to be out by New Year.'

'Where did you say you went to school?' said Tarquin. 'Near here? No, I thought not. So – er – how did you two meet?'

'That's enough, Daddy,' said Miranda. 'Come on, Colin. We need some air.'

Grabbing a duffel coat, she dragged Colin past the open-mouthed faces and ran off out of the house and into the snow, the branching shoots of melodrama sprouting enjoyably in her chest.

'Awful awful awful,' she sang, dancing ahead of him down the drive. 'I can't believe how awful they are. Escape!'

'Those crisps,' he said, shaking his head. 'Evil.' Then, 'Let's go.'

They ran together, puffing silver clouds into the icy air, down onto the main road, past the petrol station and over to the left along an overgrown lane leading to a track which took them up at last to the high fields. Here, the snow was untouched, its surface crust unbroken. They crunched to a halt at last, panting. The sun was low and red on the brow of the hill.

'They're all so crude,' she said, once her breath had come back. 'Going on at me about Aids and herpes all the time.'

'When I have children,' he began.

'I'm never going to,' she interrupted. 'They've put me off for good.'

'Don't say that,' he said.

He scooped up a fistful of the crumping snow and clasped her hands round it, then clapped his hands round hers. Inside, the snowball hardened, compacted down to the size of an egg. They stood and waited, and the ice water trickled out from between their knuckles and inter-laced fingers.

'Not much left now,' she said.

He bent his head and kissed their coupled hands, then unfastened them. There was a small icy nugget the size of a squash ball. He took it and bit it and swallowed it down.

'There,' he said. 'I'd do anything for you.'

Their faces were pink as peonies, chilled on the surface but burning just beneath the skin. They stood hugging and kissing for a few minutes, warming their hands inside each other's coats, then Colin broke free and went tearing off into a series of high jumps and somersaults, shouting, leaping at the lowest branches of the oak trees and shaking off their moss of snow.

'Why are you doing that?' called Miranda.

'Why not?' he yelled. 'Come on!' This time he took her hand and ran with her to a new untrodden clearing.

They lay down side by side on their backs and scissored their arms up and down against the snow, their legs from side to side, laughing from deep inside their stomachs. When they stood up, there were two deep winged and robed indentations. They stared at each other with snow-dazzled eyes.

At this moment in the waning day something very unusual happened. The cold air near the ground had been overlaid with a quilt of warmer air, and where the two airs kissed, so to speak, supersaturation occurred. This is quite a common event in the polar regions, though not in Hertfordshire, and Miranda and Colin stood astonished and entranced as castle-sized clouds of diamond dust floated down from the cloudless sky, a trillion ice crystals drifting and glittering in the light of the sun and the moon, to form halos, coronas, arabesques and other iridescent phenomena before their delighted gaze.

Then, very swift and silent, the last of the fabulous light trickled away. They started to shiver. Soaked in snowmelt, their wet clothes struck a chill beyond the flesh into their central bones. The dazzling crystalline pantomime had vanished into thin air, and they were left standing on a cold hill.

'Let's go,' said Colin.

They joined hands and started to run.

When at last they reached the street where Miranda lived, they stood outside the front door, doubled up and winded. Behind drawn curtains the rooms bloomed warm and domestic.

'Home and dry,' he panted.

'I don't want to go in.'

'Don't knock it. It's freezing out here.'

'But they really get me down.'

'You should feel sorry for them. They're stuck inside for good now.'

She flashed him a quick uncertain grin.

'Not like us,' he said, and they wrestled for a minute in a duffel-coated bearhug.

The front door opened onto the familiar hall with its holly-topped coat rack and ivy-wreathed telephone table, all bathed in yellow electric light.

'There you are,' said Jane in her dressing gown. Through another doorway they could see Susan, thumb in mouth, watching *Bedknobs and Broomsticks*.

'I was worried about you, darling,' said Jane.

'No need,' said Miranda.

'You're not feeling ill?'

'No. Why?'

'The fish soup,' said her mother sorrowfully. 'I thought it would be fine. Bottled in Marseille. Your father's been very ill. Both ends, I'm afraid. He's confined to the bathroom. And your grandmother was sick too, not so much, but they whisked her off to hospital overnight, just to be on the safe side. At her age. As for Jasper, he's had to forget that smart party he was going on to. He's not at all well. He's up in the spare room.'

'I'm all right,' said Susan. 'I didn't eat the stinky fish soup.'

'I missed it because I was dealing with the goose, of course,' said Jane. 'So I suppose I've got something to thank the wretched bird for. Even so, I've got a bit of a headache. It's all been a bit much. The fuss your father made! So now you're back I think I'll go to bed. See how he is.' She hitched up the hot water bottle she was carrying under her arm and wandered off towards the stairs.

'Good night,' they chorused.

Colin sat down between the two girls on the sofa and put an arm round each of them.

In front of them the television carried on regardless. A bed like a ship was speeding past mermaids and sea-horses, and its occupants were singing.

'Goody,' carolled Susan. 'Just us three.'

She turned to Colin pleadingly, and stroked his face.

'Can I do your hair in bunches?' she said.

'Christmas Is a Sad Season for the Poor'
by John Cheever

John Cheever was born in Quincy, Massachusetts, in 1912, and he went to school at Thayer Academy in South Braintree. He is the author of seven collections of stories and five novels. His first novel, *The Wapshot Chronicle*, won the 1958 National Book Award. In 1965 he received the Howells Medal for Fiction from the National Academy of Arts and Letters and in 1978 he won the National Book Critics Circle Award and the Pulitzer Prize. Shortly before his death in 1982 he was awarded the National Medal for Literature.

Read more by John Cheever:
Collected Stories
The Wapshot Chronicle
Bullet Park

Christmas is a sad season. The phrase came to Charlie an instant after the alarm clock had waked him, and named for him an amorphous depression that had troubled him all the previous evening. The sky outside his window was black. He sat up in bed and pulled the light chain that hung in front of his nose. Christmas is a very sad day of the year, he thought. Of all the millions of people in New York, I am practically the only one who has to get up in the cold black of 6 a.m. on Christmas Day in the morning; I am practically the only one.

He dressed, and when he went downstairs from the top floor of the rooming house in which he lived, the only sounds he heard were the coarse sounds of sleep; the only lights burning were lights that had been forgotten. Charlie ate some breakfast in an all-night lunchwagon and took an Elevated train uptown. From Third Avenue, he walked over to Park. Park Avenue was dark. House after house put into the shine of the street lights a wall of black windows. Millions and millions were sleeping, and this general loss of consciousness generated an impression of abandonment, as if this were the fall of the city, the end of time. He

opened the iron-and-glass doors of the apartment building where he had been working for six months as an
elevator operator, and went through the elegant lobby to
a locker room at the back. He put on a striped vest with
brass buttons, a false ascot, a pair of pants with a light-
blue stripe on the seam, and a coat. The night elevator
man was dozing on the little bench in the car. Charlie
woke him. The night elevator man told him thickly that
the day doorman had been taken sick and wouldn't be in
that day. With the doorman sick, Charlie wouldn't have
any relief for lunch, and a lot of people would expect him
to whistle for cabs.

Charlie had been on duty a few minutes when 14 rang – a
Mrs Hewing, who, he happened to know, was kind of
immoral. Mrs Hewing hadn't been to bed yet, and she got
into the elevator wearing a long dress under her fur coat.
She was followed by her two funny-looking dogs. He took
her down and watched her go out into the dark and take her
dogs to the curb. She was outside for only a few minutes.
Then she came in and he took her up to 14 again. When she
got off the elevator, she said, 'Merry Christmas, Charlie.'

'Well, it isn't much of a holiday for me, Mrs Hewing,' he
said. 'I think Christmas is a very sad season of the year. It
isn't that people around here ain't generous – I mean I got
plenty of tips – but, you see, I live alone in a furnished
room and I don't have any family or anything, and Christmas isn't much of a holiday for me.'

'I'm sorry, Charlie,' Mrs Hewing said. 'I don't have any family myself. It is kind of sad when you're alone, isn't it?' She called her dogs and followed them into her apartment. He went down.

It was quiet then, and Charlie lighted a cigarette. The heating plant in the basement encompassed the building at that hour in a regular and profound vibration, and the sullen noises of arriving steam heat began to resound, first in the lobby and then to reverberate up through all the sixteen stories, but this was a mechanical awakening, and it didn't lighten his loneliness or his petulance. The black air outside the glass doors had begun to turn blue, but the blue light seemed to have no source; it appeared in the middle of the air. It was a tearful light, and as it picked out the empty street and the long file of Christmas trees, he wanted to cry. Then a cab drove up, and the Walsers got out, drunk and dressed in evening clothes, and he took them up to their penthouse. The Walsers got him to brooding about the difference between his life in a furnished room and the lives of the people overhead. It was terrible.

Then the early churchgoers began to ring, but there were only three of these that morning. A few more went off to church at eight o'clock, but the majority of the building remained unconscious, although the smell of bacon and coffee had begun to drift into the elevator shaft.

At a little after nine, a nursemaid came down with a child. Both the nursemaid and the child had a deep tan and had just returned, he knew, from Bermuda. He had never been to Bermuda. He, Charlie, was a prisoner, confined eight hours a day to a six-by-eight elevator cage, which was confined in turn, to a sixteen-story shaft. In one building or another, he had made his living as an elevator operator for ten years. He estimated the average trip at about an eighth of a mile, and when he thought of the thousands of miles he had traveled, when he thought that he might have driven the car through the mists above the Caribbean and set it down on some coral beach in Bermuda, he held the narrowness of his travels against his passengers, as if it were not the nature of the elevator but the pressure of their lives that confined him, as if they had clipped his wings.

He was thinking about this when the DePauls, on 9, rang. They wished him a merry Christmas.

'Well, it's nice of you to think of me,' he said as they descended, 'but it isn't much of a holiday for me. Christmas is a sad season when you're poor. I live alone in a furnished room. I don't have any family.'

'Who do you have dinner with, Charlie?' Mrs DePaul asked.

'I don't have any Christmas dinner,' Charlie said. 'I just get a sandwich.'

'Oh, Charlie!' Mrs DePaul was a stout woman with an impulsive heart, and Charlie's plaint struck at her holiday mood as if she had been caught in a cloudburst. 'I do wish we could share our Christmas dinner with you, you know,' she said. 'I come from Vermont, you know, and when I was a child, you know, we always used to have a great many people at our table. The mailman, you know, and the school-teacher, and just anybody who didn't have any family of their own, you know, and I wish we could share our dinner with you the way we used to, you know, and I don't see any reason why we can't. We can't have you at the table, you know, because you couldn't leave the elevator – could you? – but just as soon as Mr DePaul has carved the goose, I'll give you a ring, and I'll arrange a tray for you, you know, and I want you to come up and at least share our Christmas dinner.'

Charlie thanked them, and their generosity surprised him, but he wondered if, with the arrival of friends and relatives, they wouldn't forget their offer.

Then old Mrs Gadshill rang, and when she wished him a merry Christmas, he hung his head.

'It isn't much of a holiday for me, Mrs Gadshill,' he said. 'Christmas is a sad season if you're poor. You see, I don't have any family. I live alone in a furnished room.'

'I don't have any family either, Charlie,' Mrs Gadshill said. She spoke with a pointed lack of petulance, but her grace was forced. 'That is, I don't have any children with me today. I have three children and seven grandchildren, but none of them can see their way to coming East for Christmas with me. Of course, I understand their problems. I know that it's difficult to travel with children during the holidays, although I always seemed to manage it when I was their age, but people feel differently, and we mustn't condemn them for the things we can't understand. But I know how you feel, Charlie. I haven't any family either. I'm just as lonely as you.'

Mrs Gadshill's speech didn't move him. Maybe she was lonely, but she had a ten-room apartment and three servants and bucks and bucks and diamonds and diamonds, and there were plenty of poor kids in the slums who would be happy at a chance at the food her cook threw away. Then he thought about poor kids. He sat down on a chair in the lobby and thought about them.

They got the worst of it. Beginning in the fall, there was all this excitement about Christmas and how it was a day for them. After Thanksgiving, they couldn't miss it. It was fixed so they couldn't miss it. The wreaths and decorations everywhere, and bells ringing, and trees in the park, and Santa Clauses on every corner and pictures in the magazines and newspapers and on every wall and window in the city told them that if they were good, they would get what they wanted. Even if they couldn't read, they couldn't miss it. They couldn't miss it even if they were blind. It got into the air the poor kids inhaled. Every time they took a walk, they'd see all the expensive toys in the store windows, and they'd write letters to Santa Claus, and their mothers and fathers would promise to mail them, and after the kids had gone to sleep, they'd burn the letters in the stove. And when it came Christmas morning, how could you explain it, how could you tell them that Santa Claus only visited the rich, that he didn't know about the good? How could you face them when all you had to give them was a balloon or a lollipop?

On the way home from work a few nights earlier, Charlie had seen a woman and a little girl going down Fifty-ninth Street. The little girl was crying. He guessed she was crying, he knew she was crying, because she'd seen all the things in the toy-store windows and couldn't understand why none of them were for her. Her mother did housework, he guessed, or maybe was a waitress, and he saw them going back to a room like his, with green walls and no heat, on Christmas Eve, to eat a can of soup. And he saw the little girl hang up her ragged stocking and fall asleep, and he saw the mother looking through her purse for something to put into the stocking – This reverie was interrupted by a bell on 11. He went up, and Mr and Mrs Fuller were waiting. When they wished him a merry Christmas, he said, 'Well, it isn't much of a holiday for me, Mrs Fuller. Christmas is a sad season when you're poor.'

'Do you have any children, Charlie?' Mrs Fuller asked.

'Four living,' he said. 'Two in the grave.' The majesty of his lie overwhelmed him. 'Mrs Leary's a cripple,' he added.

'How sad, Charlie,' Mrs Fuller said. She started out of the elevator when it reached the lobby, and then she turned. 'I want to give your children some presents,

Charlie,' she said. 'Mr Fuller and I are going to pay a call now, but when we come back, I want to give you some things for your children.'

He thanked her. Then the bell rang on 4, and he went up to get the Westons.

'It isn't much of a holiday for me,' he told them when they wished him a merry Christmas. 'Christmas is a sad season when you're poor. You see, I live alone in a furnished room.'

'Poor Charlie,' Mrs Weston said. 'I know just how you feel. During the war, when Mr Weston was away, I was all alone at Christmas. I didn't have any Christmas dinner or a tree or anything. I just scrambled myself some eggs and sat there and cried.' Mr Weston, who had gone into the lobby, called impatiently to his wife. 'I know just how you feel, Charlie,' Mrs Weston said.

By noon, the climate in the elevator shaft had changed from bacon and coffee to poultry and game, and the house, like an enormous and complex homestead, was absorbed in the preparations for a domestic feast. The children and their nursemaids had all returned from the Park. Grandmothers and aunts were arriving in limousines. Most of the people who came through the lobby were carrying packages wrapped in colored paper, and were wearing their best furs and new clothes. Charlie continued to complain to most of the tenants when they wished him a merry Christmas, changing his story from the lonely bachelor to the poor father, and back again, as his mood changed, but this outpouring of melancholy, and the sympathy it aroused, didn't make him feel any better.

At half past one, 9 rang, and when he went up, Mr DePaul was standing in the door of their apartment holding a cocktail shaker and a glass. 'Here's a little Christmas cheer, Charlie,' he said, and he poured Charlie a drink. Then a maid appeared with a tray of covered dishes, and Mrs DePaul came out of the living room. 'Merry Christmas, Charlie,' she said. 'I had Mr DePaul carve the goose early, so that you could have some, you know. I didn't want to put the dessert on the tray, because I was afraid it would melt, you know, so when we have our dessert, we'll call you.'

'And what is Christmas without presents?' Mr DePaul said, and he brought a large, flat box from the hall and laid it on top of the covered dishes.

'You people make it seem like a real Christmas to me,' Charlie said. Tears started into his eyes. 'Thank you, thank you.'

'Merry Christmas! Merry Christmas!' they called, and they watched him carry his dinner and his present into the elevator. He took the tray and the box into the locker room when he got down. On the tray, there was a soup, some kind of creamed fish and a serving of goose. The bell rang again, but before he answered it, he tore open the DePauls' box and saw that it held a dressing gown. Their generosity and their cocktail had begun to work on his brain, and he went jubilantly up to 12. Mrs Gadshill's maid was standing in the door with a tray, and Mrs Gadshill stood behind her. 'Merry Christmas, Charlie!' she said. He thanked her, and tears came into his eyes again. On the way down, he drank off the glass of sherry on Mrs Gadshill's tray. Mrs Gadshill's contribution was a mixed grill. He ate the lamb chop with his fingers. The bell was ringing again, and he wiped his face with a paper towel and went up to 11. 'Merry Christmas, Charlie,' Mrs Fuller said, and she was standing in the door with her arms full of packages wrapped in silver paper, just like a picture in an advertisement, and Mr Fuller was beside her with an arm around her, and they both looked as if they were going to cry. 'Here are some things I want you to take home to your children,' Mrs Fuller said. 'And here's something for Mrs Leary and here's something for you. And if you want to take these things out to the elevator, we'll have your dinner ready for you in a minute.' He carried the things into the elevator and came back for the tray. 'Merry Christmas, Charlie!' both of the Fullers called after him as he closed the door. He took their dinner and their presents into the locker room and tore open the box that was marked for him. There was an alligator wallet in it, with Mr Fuller's initials in the corner. Their dinner was also goose, and he ate a piece of the meat with his fingers and was washing it down with a cocktail when the bell rang. He went up again. This time it was the Westons. 'Merry Christmas, Charlie!' they said, and they gave him a cup of eggnog, a turkey dinner, and a present.

Their gift was also a dressing gown. Then 7 rang, and when he went up, there was another dinner and some more toys. Then 14 rang, and when he went up, Mrs Hewing was standing in the hall, in a kind of negligee, holding a pair of riding boots in one hand and some neckties in the other. She had been crying and drinking. 'Merry Christmas, Charlie,' she said tenderly. 'I wanted to give you something, and I've been thinking about you all morning, and I've been all over the apartment, and these are the only things I could find that a man might want. These are the only things that Mr Brewer left. I don't suppose you'd have any use for the riding boots, but wouldn't you like the neckties?' Charlie took the neckties and thanked her and hurried back to the car, for the elevator bell had rung three times.

By three o'clock, Charlie had fourteen dinners spread on the table and the floor of the locker room, and the bell kept ringing. Just as he started to eat one, he would have to go up and get another, and he was in the middle of the Parsons' roast beef when he had to go up and get the DePauls' dessert. He kept the door of the locker room closed, for he sensed that the quality of charity is exclusive and that his friends would have been disappointed to find that they were not the only ones to try to lessen his loneliness. There were goose, turkey, chicken, pheasant, grouse, and pigeon. There were trout and salmon, creamed scallops and oysters, lobster, crabmeat, whitebait, and clams. There were plum puddings, mince pies, mousses, puddles of melted ice cream, layer cakes, *Torten*, éclairs, and two slices of Bavarian cream. He had dressing gowns, neckties, cuff links, socks, and handkerchiefs, and one of the tenants had asked for his neck size and then given him three green shirts. There were a glass teapot filled, the label said, with jasmine honey, four bottles of aftershave lotion, some alabaster bookends, and a dozen steak knives. The avalanche of charity he had precipitated filled the locker room and made him hesitant, now and then, as if he had touched some wellspring in the female heart that would bury him alive in food and dressing gowns. He had made almost no headway on the food, for all the servings were preternaturally large, as if loneliness had been counted on to generate in him a brutish appetite. Nor had he opened any of the presents that had been given to him for his imaginary children, but he had drunk everything they sent down, and around him were the dregs of Martinis, Manhattans, Old-Fashioneds, champagne-and-raspberry shrub cocktails, eggnogs, Bronxes, and Side Cars.

His face was blazing. He loved the world, and the world loved him. When he thought back over his life, it appeared to him in a rich and wonderful light, full of astonishing experiences and unusual friends. He thought that his job as an elevator operator – cruising up and down through hundreds of feet of perilous space – demanded the nerve and the intellect of a birdman. All the constraints of his life – the green walls of his room and the months of unemployment – dissolved. No one was ringing, but he got into the elevator and shot it at full speed up to the penthouse and down again, up and down, to test his wonderful mastery of space.

A bell rang on 12 while he was cruising, and he stopped in his flight long enough to pick up Mrs Gadshill. As the car started to fall, he took his hands off the controls in a paroxysm of joy and shouted, 'Strap on your safety belt, Mrs Gadshill! We're going to make a loop-the-loop!' Mrs Gadshill shrieked. Then, for some reason, she sat down on the floor of the elevator. Why was her face so pale, he wondered; why was she sitting on the floor? She shrieked again. He grounded the car gently, and cleverly, he thought, and opened the door. 'I'm sorry if I scared you, Mrs Gadshill,' he said meekly. 'I was only fooling.' She shrieked again. Then she ran out into the lobby, screaming for the superintendent.

The superintendent fired Charlie and took over the elevator himself. The news that he was out of work stung Charlie for a minute. It was his first contact with human meanness that day. He sat down in the locker room and gnawed on a drumstick. His drinks were beginning to let him down, and while it had not reached him yet, he felt a miserable soberness in the offing. The excess of food and presents around him began to make him feel guilty and unworthy. He regretted bitterly the lie he had told about his children. He was a single man with simple needs. He had abused the goodness of the people upstairs. He was unworthy.

Then up through this drunken train of thought surged the sharp figure of his landlady and her three skinny children. He thought of them sitting in their basement room. The cheer of Christmas had passed them by. This image got him to his feet. The realization that he was in a position to give, that he could bring happiness easily to someone else, sobered him. He took a big burlap sack, which was used for collecting waste, and began to stuff it, first with his presents and then with the presents for his imaginary children. He worked with the haste of a man whose train is approaching the station, for he could hardly wait to see those long faces light up when he came in the door. He changed his clothes, and, fired by a wonderful and unfamiliar sense of power, he slung his bag over his shoulder like a regular Santa Claus, went out the back way, and took a taxi to the lower East Side.

The landlady and her children had just finished off a turkey, which had been sent to them by the local Democratic Club, and they were stuffed and uncomfortable when Charlie began pounding on the door, shouting 'Merry Christmas!' He dragged the bag in after him and dumped the presents for the children onto the floor. There were dolls and musical toys, blocks, sewing kits, an Indian suit, and a loom, and it appeared to him that, as he had hoped, his arrival in the basement dispelled its gloom. When half the presents had been opened, he gave the landlady a bathrobe and went upstairs to look over the things he had been given for himself.

Now, the landlady's children had already received so many presents by the time Charlie arrived that they were confused with receiving, and it was only the landlady's intuitive grasp of the nature of charity that made her allow the children to open some of the presents while Charlie was still in the room, but as soon as he had gone, she stood between the children and the presents that were still unopened. 'Now, you kids have had enough already,' she said. 'You kids have got your share. Just look at the things you got there. Why, you ain't even played with the half of them. Mary Anne, you ain't even looked at that doll the Fire Department give you. Now, a nice thing to do would be to take all this stuff that's left over to those poor people on Hudson Street – them Deckkers. They ain't got nothing.' A beatific light came into her face when she realized that she could give, that she could bring cheer, that she could put a healing finger on a case needier than hers, and – like Mrs DePaul and Mrs Weston, like Charlie himself and like Mrs Deckker, when Mrs Deckker was to think, subsequently, of the poor Shannons – first love, then charity, and then a sense of power drove her. 'Now, you kids help me get all this stuff together. Hurry, hurry, hurry,' she said, for it was dark then, and she knew that we are bound, one to another, in licentious benevolence for only a single day, and that day was nearly over. She was tired, but she couldn't rest, she couldn't rest.

'A Serious Talk'
by Raymond Carver

Raymond Carver was born in Oregon in 1938. His father was a saw-mill worker and his mother was a waitress and clerk. He married early and for years writing had to come second to earning a living for his young family. It was not until *Will You Please Be Quiet Please?* appeared in 1976 that his work began to reach a wider audience. This was the year in which he gave up alcohol, which had contributed to the collapse of his marriage. In 1977 he met the writer Tess Gallagher, with whom he shared the last eleven years of his life. During this prolific period he wrote three collections of stories, *Fires*, a collection of essays, poems and stories, and three further collections of poetry. Raymond Carver died in 1988.

Read more by Raymond Carver:
What We Talk About When We Talk About Love
Cathedral
Elephant

Vera's car was there, no others, and Burt gave thanks for that. He pulled into the drive and stopped beside the pie he'd dropped the night before. It was still there, the aluminum pan upside down, a halo of pumpkin filling on the pavement. It was the day after Christmas.

He'd come on Christmas day to visit his wife and children. Vera had warned him beforehand. She'd told him the score. She'd said he had to be out by six o'clock because her friend and his children were coming for dinner.

They had sat in the living room and solemnly opened the presents Burt had brought over. They had opened his packages while other packages wrapped in festive paper lay piled under the tree waiting for after six o'clock.

He had watched the children open their gifts, waited while Vera undid the ribbon on hers. He saw her slip off the paper, lift the lid, take out the cashmere sweater.

'It's nice,' she said. 'Thank you, Burt.'

'Try it on,' his daughter said.

'Put it on,' his son said.

Burt looked at his son, grateful for his backing him up.

She did try it on. Vera went into the bedroom and came out with it on.

'It's nice,' she said.

'It's nice on *you*,' Burt said, and felt a welling in his chest.

He opened his gifts. From Vera, a gift certificate at Sondheim's men's store. From his daughter, a matching comb and brush. From his son, a ballpoint pen.

Vera served sodas, and they did a little talking. But mostly they looked at the tree. Then his daughter got up and began setting the dining-room table, and his son went off to his room.

But Burt liked it where he was. He liked it in front of the fireplace, a glass in his hand, his house, his home.

Then Vera went into the kitchen.

From time to time his daughter walked into the dining room with something for the table. Burt watched her. He watched her fold the linen napkins into the wine glasses. He watched her put a slender vase in the middle of the table. He watched her lower a flower into the vase, doing it ever so carefully.

A small wax and sawdust log burned on the grate. A carton of five more sat ready on the hearth. He got up from the sofa and put them all in the fireplace. He watched until they flamed. Then he finished his soda and made for the patio door. On the way, he saw the pies lined up on the sideboard. He stacked them in his arms, all six, one for every ten times she had ever betrayed him.

In the driveway in the dark, he'd let one fall as he fumbled with the door.

The front door was permanently locked since the night his key had broken off inside it. He went around to the back. There was a wreath on the patio door. He rapped on the glass. Vera was in her bathrobe. She looked out at him and frowned. She opened the door a little.

Burt said, 'I want to apologize to you for last night. I want to apologize to the kids, too.'

Vera said, 'They're not here.'

She stood in the doorway and he stood on the patio next to the philodendron plant. He pulled at some lint on his sleeve.

She said, 'I can't take any more. You tried to burn the house down.'

'I did not.'

'You did. Everybody here was a witness.'

He said, 'Can I come in and talk about it?'

She drew the robe together at her throat and moved back inside.

She said, 'I have to go somewhere in an hour.'

He looked around. The tree blinked on and off. There was a pile of colored tissue paper and shiny boxes at one end of the sofa. A turkey carcass sat on a platter in the center of the dining-room table, the leathery remains in a bed of parsley as if in a horrible nest. A cone of ash filled the fireplace. There were some empty Shasta cola cans in there too. A trail of smoke stains rose up the bricks to the mantel, where the wood that stopped them was scorched black.

He turned around and went back to the kitchen.

He said, 'What time did your friend leave last night?'

She said, 'If you're going to start that, you can go right now.'

He pulled a chair out and sat down at the kitchen table in front of the big ashtray. He closed his eyes and opened them. He moved the curtain aside and looked out at the backyard. He saw a bicycle without a front wheel standing upside down. He saw weeds growing along the redwood fence.

She ran water into a saucepan. 'Do you remember Thanksgiving?' she said. 'I said then that was the last holiday you were going to wreck for us. Eating bacon and eggs instead of turkey at ten o'clock at night.'

'I know it,' he said. 'I said I'm sorry.'

'Sorry isn't good enough.'

The pilot light was out again. She was at the stove trying to get the gas going under the pan of water.

'Don't burn yourself,' he said. 'Don't catch yourself on fire.'

He considered her robe catching fire, him jumping up from the table, throwing her down onto the floor and rolling her over and over into the living room, where he would cover her with his body. Or should he run to the bedroom for a blanket?

'Vera?'

She looked at him.

'Do you have anything to drink? I could use a drink this morning.'

'There's some vodka in the freezer.'

'When did you start keeping vodka in the freezer?'

'Don't ask.'

'Okay,' he said, 'I won't ask.'

He got out the vodka and poured some into a cup he found on the counter.

She said, 'Are you just going to drink it like that, out of a cup?' she said. 'Jesus, Burt. What'd you want to talk about, anyway? I told you I have someplace to go. I have a flute lesson at one o'clock.'

'Are you still taking flute?'

'I just said so. What is it? Tell me what's on your mind, and then I have to get ready.'

'I wanted to say I was sorry.'

She said, 'You said that.'

He said, 'If you have any juice, I'll mix it with this vodka.'

She opened the refrigerator and moved things around.

'There's cranapple juice,' she said.

'That's fine,' he said.

'I'm going to the bathroom,' she said.

He drank the cup of cranapple juice and vodka. He lit a cigarette and tossed the match into the big ashtray that always sat on the kitchen table. He studied the butts in it. Some of them were Vera's brand, and some of them weren't. Some even were lavender-colored. He got up and dumped it all under the sink.

The ashtray was not really an ashtray. It was a big dish of stoneware they'd bought from a bearded potter on the mall in Santa Clara. He rinsed it out and dried it. He put it back on the table. And then he ground out his cigarette in it.

The water on the stove began to bubble just as the phone began to ring.

He heard her open the bathroom door and call to him through the living room. 'Answer that! I'm about to get into the shower.'

The kitchen phone was on the counter in a corner behind the roasting pan. He moved the roasting pan and picked up the receiver.

'Is Charlie there?' the voice said.

'No,' Burt said.

'Okay,' the voice said.

While he was seeing to the coffee, the phone rang again.

'Charlie?'

'Not here,' Burt said.

This time he left the receiver off the hook.

*

Vera came back into the kitchen wearing jeans and a sweater and brushing her hair.

He spooned the instant into the cups of hot water and then spilled some vodka into his. He carried the cups over to the table.

She picked up the receiver, listened. She said, 'What's this? Who was on the phone?'

'Nobody,' he said. 'Who smokes colored cigarettes?'

'I do.'

'I didn't know you did that.'

'Well, I *do*.'

She sat across from him and drank her coffee. They smoked and used the ashtray.

There were things he wanted to say, grieving things, consoling things, things like that.

'I'm smoking three packs a day,' Vera said. 'I mean, if you really want to know what goes on around here.'

'God almighty,' Burt said.

Vera nodded.

'I didn't come over here to hear that,' he said.

'What did you come over here to hear, then? You want to hear the house burned down?'

'Vera,' he said. 'It's Christmas. That's why I came.'

'It's the day after Christmas,' she said. 'Christmas has come and gone,' she said. 'I don't ever want to see another one.'

'What about me?' he said. 'You think I look forward to holidays?'

*

The phone rang again. Burt picked it up.

'It's someone wanting Charlie,' he said.

'What?'

'Charlie,' Burt said.

Vera took the phone. She kept her back to him as she talked. Then she turned to him and said, 'I'll take this call in the bedroom. So would you please hang up after I've picked it up in there? I can tell, so hang it up when I say.'

He took the receiver. She left the kitchen. He held the receiver to his ear and listened. He heard nothing. Then he heard a man clear his throat. Then he heard Vera pick up the other phone. She shouted, 'Okay, Burt! I have it now, Burt!'

He put down the receiver and stood looking at it. He opened the silverware drawer and pushed things around inside. He opened another drawer. He looked in the sink. He went into the dining room and got the carving knife. He held it under hot water until the grease broke and ran off. He wiped the blade on his sleeve. He moved to the phone, doubled the cord, and sawed through without any trouble at all. He examined the ends of the cord. Then he shoved the phone back into its corner behind the roasting pan.

She came in. She said, 'The phone went dead. Did you do anything to the telephone?' She looked at the phone and then picked it up from the counter.

'Son of a bitch!' she screamed. She screamed, 'Out, out,

where you belong!' She was shaking the phone at him. 'That's it! I'm going to get a restraining order, that's what I'm going to get!'

The phone made a *ding* when she banged it down on the counter.

'I'm going next door to call the police if you don't get out of here now!'

He picked up the ashtray. He held it by its edge. He posed with it like a man preparing to hurl the discus.

'Please,' she said. 'That's our ashtray.'

He left through the patio door. He was not certain, but he thought he had proved something. He hoped he had made something clear. The thing was, they had to have a serious talk soon. There were things that needed talking about, important things that had to be discussed. They'd talk again. Maybe after the holidays were over and things got back to normal. He'd tell her the goddamn ashtray was a goddamn dish, for example.

He stepped around the pie in the driveway and got back into his car. He started the car and put it into reverse. It was hard managing until he put the ashtray down.

'The Adventure of the Blue Carbuncle'
by Arthur Conan Doyle

Sir Arthur Conan Doyle was born on 22 May 1859 in Edinburgh. He studied medicine at the University of Edinburgh and began to write stories while he was a student. Over his life he produced more than thirty books, 150 short stories, poems, plays and essays across a wide range of genres. His most famous creation is the detective Sherlock Holmes, who he introduced in his first novel, *A Study in Scarlet* (1887). This was followed in 1889 by a historical novel, *Micah Clarke.* In 1893 Conan Doyle published 'The Final Problem' in which he killed off his famous detective so that he could turn his attention more towards historical fiction. However Holmes was so popular that Conan Doyle eventually relented and published *The Hound of the Baskervilles* in 1902, followed by many more Sherlock Holmes stories, until he was finally retired in 1927. Sir Arthur Conan Doyle died on 7 July 1930.

Read more by Arthur Conan Doyle:
The Complete Sherlock Holmes
The Lost World

I had called upon my friend Sherlock Holmes upon the second morning after Christmas, with the intention of wishing him the compliments of the season. He was lounging upon the sofa in a purple dressing-gown, a pipe-rack within his reach upon the right, and a pile of crumpled morning papers, evidently newly studied, near at hand. Beside the couch was a wooden chair, and on the angle of the back hung a very seedy and disreputable hard felt hat, much the worse for wear, and cracked in several places. A lens and a forceps lying upon the seat of the chair suggested that the hat had been suspended in this manner for the purpose of examination.

'You are engaged,' said I; 'perhaps I interrupt you.'

'Not at all. I am glad to have a friend with whom I can discuss my results. The matter is a perfectly trivial one' (he jerked his thumb in the direction of the old hat), 'but there are points in connection with it which are not entirely devoid of interest, and even of instruction.'

I seated myself in his armchair, and warmed my hands before his crackling fire, for a sharp frost had set in, and the windows were thick with the ice crystals. 'I suppose,' I remarked, 'that, homely as it looks, this thing has some deadly story linked on to it – that it is the clue which will guide you in the solution of some mystery, and the punishment of some crime.'

'No, no. No crime,' said Sherlock Holmes, laughing. 'Only one of those whimsical little incidents which will happen when you have four million human beings all jostling each other within the space of a few square miles. Amid the action and reaction of so dense a swarm of humanity, every possible combination of events may be expected to take place, and many a little problem will be presented which may be striking and bizarre without being criminal. We have already had experience of such.'

'So much so,' I remarked, 'that, of the last six cases which I have added to my notes, three have been entirely free of any legal crime.'

'Precisely. You allude to my attempt to recover the Irene Adler papers, to the singular case of Miss Mary Sutherland, and to the adventure of the man with the twisted lip. Well, I have no doubt that this small matter will fall into the same innocent category. You know Peterson, the commissionaire?'

'Yes.'

'It is to him that this trophy belongs.'

'It is his hat.'

'No, no; he found it. Its owner is unknown. I beg that you will look upon it, not as a battered billycock, but as an intellectual problem. And, first, as to how it came here. It arrived upon Christmas morning, in company with a good fat goose, which is, I have no doubt, roasting at this moment in front of Peterson's fire. The facts are these. About four o'clock on Christmas morning, Peterson, who, as you know, is a very honest fellow, was returning from some small jollification, and was making his way homewards down Tottenham Court-road. In front of him he saw, in the gaslight, a tallish man, walking with a slight stagger, and carrying a white goose slung over his shoulder. As he reached the corner of Goodge-street, a row broke out between this stranger and a little knot of roughs. One of the latter knocked off the man's hat, on which he raised his stick to defend himself, and, swinging it over his head, smashed the shop window behind him. Peterson had rushed forward to protect the stranger from his assailants, but the man, shocked at having broken the window, and seeing an official-looking person in uniform rushing towards him, dropped his goose, took to his heels, and vanished amid the labyrinth of small streets which lie at the back of Tottenham Court-road. The roughs had also fled at the appearance of Peterson, so that he was left in possession of the field of battle, and also of the spoils of victory in the shape of this battered hat and a most unimpeachable Christmas goose.'

'Which surely he restored to their owner?'

'My dear fellow, there lies the problem. It is true that "For Mrs Henry Baker" was printed upon a small card which was tied to the bird's left leg, and it is also true that the initials "H.B." are legible upon the lining of this hat; but, as there are some thousands of Bakers, and some hundreds of Henry Bakers in this city of ours, it is not easy to restore lost property to any one of them.'

'What, then, did Peterson do?'

'He brought round both hat and goose to me on Christmas morning, knowing that even the smallest problems are of interest to me. The goose we retained until this morning, when there were signs that, in spite of the slight frost, it would be well that it should be eaten without unnecessary delay. Its finder has carried it off, therefore, to fulfil the ultimate destiny of a goose, while I continue to retain the hat of the unknown gentleman who lost his Christmas dinner.'

'Did he not advertise?'

'No.'

'Then, what clue could you have as to his identity?'

'Only as much as we can deduce.'

'From his hat?'

'Precisely.'

'But you are joking. What can you gather from this old battered felt?'

'Here is my lens. You know my methods. What can you gather your self as to the individuality of the man who has worn this article?'

I took the tattered object in my hands, and turned it over rather ruefully. It was a very ordinary black hat of the usual round shape, hard, and much the worse for wear. The lining had been of red silk, but was a good deal discoloured. There was no maker's name; but, as Holmes had remarked, the initials 'H.B.' were scrawled upon one side. It was pierced in the brim for a hat-securer, but the elastic was missing. For the rest, it was cracked, exceedingly dusty, and spotted in several places, although there seemed to have been some attempt to hide the discoloured patches by smearing them with ink.

'I can see nothing,' said I, handing it back to my friend.

'On the contrary, Watson, you can see everything. You fail, however, to reason from what you see. You are too timid in drawing your inferences.'

'Then, pray tell me what it is that you can infer from this hat?'

He picked it up, and gazed at it in the peculiar introspective fashion which was characteristic of him. 'It is perhaps less suggestive than it might have been,' he remarked, 'and yet there are a few inferences which are very distinct, and a few others which represent at least a strong balance of probability. That the man was highly intellectual is of course obvious upon the face of it, and also that he was fairly well-to-do within the last three years, although he has now fallen upon evil days. He had foresight, but has less now than formerly, pointing to a moral retrogression, which, when taken with the decline of his fortunes, seems to indicate some evil influence, probably drink, at work upon him. This may account also for the obvious fact that his wife has ceased to love him.'

'My dear Holmes!'

'He has, however, retained some degree of self-respect,' he continued, disregarding my remonstrance. 'He is a man who leads a sedentary life, goes out little, is out of training entirely, is middle-aged, has grizzled hair which he has had cut within the last few days, and which he anoints with lime-cream. These are the more patent facts which are to be deduced from his hat. Also, by the way, that it is extremely improbable that he has gas laid on in his house.'

'You are certainly joking, Holmes.'

'Not in the least. Is it possible that even now when I give you these results you are unable to see how they are attained?'

'I have no doubt that I am very stupid; but I must confess that I am unable to follow you. For example, how did you deduce that this man was intellectual?'

For answer Holmes clapped the hat upon his head. It came right over the forehead and settled upon the bridge of his nose. 'It is a question of cubic capacity,' said he; 'a man with so large a brain must have something in it.'

'The decline of his fortunes, then?'

'This hat is three years old. These flat brims curled at the edge came in then. It is a hat of the very best quality. Look at the band of ribbed silk, and the excellent lining. If this man could afford to buy so expensive a hat three years ago, and has had no hat since, then he has assuredly gone down in the world.'

'Well, that is clear enough, certainly. But how about the foresight, and the moral retrogression?'

Sherlock Holmes laughed. 'Here is the foresight,' said he, putting his finger upon the little disc and loop of the hat-securer. 'They are never sold upon hats. If this man ordered one, it is a sign of a certain amount of fore-sight, since he went out of his way to take this precaution against the wind. But since we see that he has broken the elastic, and has not troubled to replace it, it is obvious that he has less foresight now than formerly, which is a distinct proof of a weakening nature. On the other hand, he has endeavoured to conceal some of these stains upon the felt by daubing them with ink, which is a sign that he has not entirely lost his self-respect.'

'Your reasoning is certainly plausible.'

'The further points, that he is middle-aged, that his hair is grizzled, that it has been recently cut, and that he uses lime-cream, are all to be gathered from a close examination of the lower part of the lining. The lens discloses a large number of hair ends, clean cut by the scissors of the barber. They all appear to be adhesive, and there is a distinct odour of lime-cream. This dust, you will observe, is not the gritty, grey dust of the street, but the fluffy brown dust of the house, showing that it has been hung up indoors most of the time; while the marks of moisture

upon the inside are proof positive that the wearer per-
spired very freely, and could, therefore, hardly be in the
best of training.'

'But his wife – you said that she had ceased to love him.'

'This hat has not been brushed for weeks. When I see
you, my dear Watson, with a week's accumulation of dust
upon your hat, and when your wife allows you to go out in
such a state, I shall fear that you also have been unfortunate enough to lose your wife's affection.'

'But he might be a bachelor.'

'Nay, he was bringing home the goose as a peace-
offering to his wife. Remember the card upon the bird's
leg.'

'You have an answer to everything. But how on earth
do you deduce that the gas is not laid on in the house?'

'One tallow stain, or even two, might come by chance;
but, when I see no less than five, I think that there can be
little doubt that the individual must be brought into frequent contact with burning tallow – walks upstairs at
night probably with his hat in one hand and a guttering
candle in the other. Anyhow, he never got tallow stains
from a gas jet. Are you satisfied?'

'Well, it is very ingenious,' said I, laughing; 'but since,
as you said just now, there has been no crime committed,
and no harm done save the loss of a goose, all this seems
to be rather a waste of energy.'

Sherlock Holmes had opened his mouth to reply, when
the door flew open, and Peterson the commissionaire

rushed into the apartment with flushed cheeks and the face of a man who is dazed with astonishment.

'The goose, Mr Holmes! The goose, sir!' he gasped.

'Eh? What of it, then? Has it returned to life, and flapped off through the kitchen window?' Holmes twisted himself round upon the sofa to get a fairer view of the man's excited face.

'See here, sir! See what my wife found in its crop!' He held out his hand, and displayed upon the centre of the palm a brilliantly scintillating blue stone, rather smaller than a bean in size, but of such purity and radiance that it twinkled like an electric point in the dark hollow of his hand.

Sherlock Holmes sat up with a whistle. 'By Jove, Peterson!' said he, 'this is treasure trove indeed. I suppose you know what you have got?'

'A diamond, sir! A precious stone! It cuts into glass as though it were putty.'

'It's more than a precious stone. It's *the* precious stone.'

'Not the Countess of Morcar's blue carbuncle!' I ejaculated.

'Precisely so. I ought to know its size and shape, seeing that I have read the advertisement about it in *The Times* every day lately. It is absolutely unique, and its value can only be conjectured, but the reward offered of a thousand pounds is certainly not within a twentieth part of the market price.'

'A thousand pounds! Great Lord of mercy!' The commissionaire plumped down into a chair, and stared from one to the other of us.

'That is the reward, and I have reason to know that there are sentimental considerations in the background which would induce the Countess to part with half of her fortune, if she could but recover the gem.'

'It was lost, if I remember aright, at the Hotel Cosmopolitan,' I remarked.

'Precisely so, on the twenty-second of December, just five days ago. John Horner, a plumber, was accused of having abstracted it from the lady's jewel case. The evidence against him was so strong that the case has been referred to the Assizes. I have some account of the matter here, I believe.' He rummaged amid his newspapers, glancing over the dates, until at last he smoothed one out, doubled it over, and read the following paragraph:

"Hotel Cosmopolitan Jewel Robbery. John Horner, 26, plumber, was brought up upon the charge of having upon the 22nd inst. abstracted from the jewel case of the Countess of Morcar the valuable gem known as the blue carbuncle. James Ryder, upper-attendant at the hotel, gave his evidence to the effect that he had shown Horner up to the dressing-room of the Countess of Morcar upon the day of the robbery, in order that he might solder the second bar of the grate, which was loose. He had remained with Horner some little time, but had finally been called away. On returning, he found that Horner had disappeared, that the bureau had been forced open, and that the small morocco casket in which, as it afterwards transpired, the Countess was accustomed to keep her jewel was lying empty upon the dressing-table. Ryder instantly gave the alarm, and Horner was arrested the same evening; but the stone could not be found either upon his person or in his rooms. Catherine Cusack, maid to the Countess, deposed to having heard Ryder's cry of dismay on discovering the robbery, and to having rushed into the room, where she found matters as described by the last witness. Inspector Bradstreet, B division, gave evidence as to the arrest of Horner, who struggled frantically, and protested his innocence in the strongest terms. Evidence of a previous conviction for robbery having been given against the prisoner, the magistrate refused to deal summarily with the offence, but referred it to the Assizes. Horner, who had shown signs of intense emotion during the proceedings, fainted away at the conclusion, and was carried out of court."

'Hum! So much for the police-court,' said Holmes, thoughtfully, tossing aside the paper. 'The question for us now to solve is the sequence of events leading from a rifled jewel case at one end to the crop of a goose in Tottenham Court-road at the other. You see, Watson, our little deductions have suddenly assumed a much more important and less innocent aspect. Here is the stone; the stone came from the goose, and the goose came from Mr Henry Baker, the gentleman with the bad hat and all the other characteristics with which I have bored you. So now we must set ourselves very seriously to finding this gentleman, and ascertaining what part he has played in this little mystery. To do this, we must try the simplest means first, and these lie undoubtedly in an advertisement in all the evening papers. If this fail, I shall have recourse to other methods.'

'What will you say?'

'Give me a pencil, and that slip of paper. Now then: "Found at the corner of Goodge-street, a goose and a black felt hat. Mr Henry Baker can have the same by applying at 6.30 this evening at 221B, Baker-street." That is clear and concise.'

'Very. But will he see it?'

'Well, he is sure to keep an eye on the papers, since, to a poor man, the loss was a heavy one. He was clearly so scared by his mischance in breaking the window, and by the approach of Peterson, that he thought of nothing but flight; but since then he must have bitterly regretted the impulse which caused him to drop his bird. Then, again, the introduction of his name will cause him to see it, for every one who knows him will direct his attention to it. Here you are Peterson, run down to the advertising agency, and have this put in the evening papers.'

'In which, sir?'

'Oh, in the *Globe, Star, Pall Mall, St Fames's Gazette, Evening News, Standard, Echo*, and any others that occur to you.'

'Very well, sir. And this stone?'

'Ah, yes, I shall keep the stone. Thank you. And, I say, Peterson, just buy a goose on your way back, and leave it here with me, for we must have one to give to this gentleman in place of the one which your family is now devouring.'

When the commissionaire had gone, Holmes took up the stone and held it against the light. 'It's a bonny thing,' said he. 'Just see how it glints and sparkles. Of course it is a nucleus and focus of crime. Every good stone is. They are the devil's pet baits. In the larger and older jewels every facet may stand for a bloody deed. This stone is not yet twenty years old. It was found in the banks of the Amoy River in Southern China, and is remarkable in having every characteristic of the carbuncle, save that it is blue in shade, instead of ruby red. In spite of its youth, it has already a sinister history. There have been two murders, a vitriol-throwing, a suicide, and several robberies brought about for the sake of this forty-grain weight of crystallised charcoal. Who would think that so pretty a toy would be a purveyor to the gallows and the prison? I'll lock it up in my strong-box now, and drop a line to the Countess to say that we have it.'

'Do you think this man Horner is innocent?'

'I cannot tell.'

'Well, then, do you imagine that this other one, Henry Baker, had anything to do with the matter?'

'It is, I think, much more likely that Henry Baker is an absolutely innocent man, who had no idea that the bird which he was carrying was of considerably more value than if it were made of solid gold. That, however, I shall determine by a very simple test, if we have an answer to our advertisement.'

'And you can do nothing until then?'

'Nothing.'

'In that case I shall continue my professional round. But I shall come back in the evening at the hour you have mentioned, for I should like to see the solution of so tangled a business.'

'Very glad to see you. I dine at seven. There is a woodcock, I believe. By the way, in view of recent occurrences, perhaps I ought to ask Mrs Hudson to examine its crop.'

I had been delayed at a case, and it was a little after half-past six when I found myself in Baker-street once more. As I approached the house I saw a tall man in a Scotch bonnet, with a coat which was buttoned up to his chin, waiting outside in the bright semicircle which was thrown from the fanlight. Just as I arrived, the door was opened, and we were shown up together to Holmes' room.

'Mr Henry Baker, I believe,' said he, rising from his armchair, and greeting his visitor with the easy air of geniality which he could so readily assume. 'Pray take this chair by the fire, Mr Baker. It is a cold night, and I observe that your circulation is more adapted for summer than for winter. Ah, Watson, you have just come at the right time. Is that your hat, Mr Baker?'

'Yes, sir, that is undoubtedly my hat.'

He was a large man, with rounded shoulders, a massive head, and a broad, intelligent face, sloping down to a pointed beard of grizzled brown. A touch of red in nose and cheeks, with a slight tremor of his extended hand, recalled Holmes' surmise as to his habits. His rusty black frock-coat was buttoned right up in front, with the collar turned up, and his lank wrists protruded from his sleeves without a sign of cuff or shirt. He spoke in a low staccato fashion, choosing his words with care, and gave the impression generally of a man of learning and letters who had had ill-usage at the hands of fortune.

'We have retained these things for some days,' said Holmes, 'because we expected to see an advertisement from you giving your address. I am at a loss to know now why you did not advertise.'

Our visitor gave a rather shame-faced laugh. 'Shillings have not been so plentiful with me as they once were,' he remarked. 'I had no doubt that the gang of roughs who assaulted me had carried off both my hat and the bird. I did not care to spend more money in a hopeless attempt at recovering them.'

'Very naturally. By the way, about the bird, we were compelled to eat it.'

'To eat it!' Our visitor half rose from his chair in his excitement.

'Yes, it would have been no use to any one had we not done so. But I presume that this other goose upon the sideboard, which is about the same weight and perfectly fresh, will answer your purpose equally well?'

'Oh, certainly, certainly!' answered Mr Baker, with a sigh of relief.

'Of course, we still have the feathers, legs, crop, and so on of your own bird, so if you wish–'

The man burst into a hearty laugh. 'They might be useful to me as relics of my adventure,' said he, 'but beyond that I can hardly see what use the *disjecta membra* of my late acquaintance are going to be to me. No, sir, I think that, with your permission, I will confine my attentions to the excellent bird which I perceive upon the sideboard.'

Sherlock Holmes glanced sharply across at me with a slight shrug of his shoulders.

'There is your hat, then, and there your bird,' said he. 'By the way, would it bore you to tell me where you got the other one from? I am somewhat of a fowl fancier, and I have seldom seen a better-grown goose.'

'Certainly, sir,' said Baker, who had risen and tucked his newly-gained property under his arm. 'There are a few of us who frequent the "Alpha" Inn, near the Museum – we are to be found in the Museum itself during the day, you understand. This year our good host, Windigate by name, instituted a goose club, by which, on consideration of some few pence every week, we were each to receive a bird at Christmas. My pence were duly paid, and the rest is familiar to you. I am much indebted to you, sir, for a Scotch bonnet is fitted neither to my years nor my gravity.' With a comical pomposity of manner he bowed solemnly to both of us, and strode off upon his way.

'So much for Mr Henry Baker,' said Holmes, when he had closed the door behind him. 'It is quite certain that he knows nothing whatever about the matter. Are you hungry, Watson?'

'Not particularly.'

'Then I suggest that we turn our dinner into a supper, and follow up this clue while it is still hot.'

'By all means.'

It was a bitter night, so we drew on our ulsters and wrapped cravats about our throats. Outside, the stars were shining coldly in a cloudless sky, and the breath of the passers-by blew out into smoke like so many pistol shots. Our footfalls rang out crisply and loudly as we swung through the Doctors' quarter, Wimpole-street, Harley-street, and so through Wigmore-street into Oxford-street. In a quarter of an hour we were in Blooms-bury at the "Alpha" Inn, which is a small public-house at the corner of one of the streets which runs down into Hol-born. Holmes pushed open the door of the private bar, and ordered two glasses of beer from the ruddy-faced, white-aproned landlord.

'Your beer should be excellent if it is as good as your geese,' said he.

'My geese!' The man seemed surprised.

'Yes. I was speaking only half an hour ago to Mr Henry Baker, who was a member of your goose-club.'

'Ah! yes, I see. But you see, sir, them's not *our* geese.'

'Indeed! Whose, then?'

'Well, I got the two dozen from a salesman in Covent Garden.'

'Indeed! I know some of them. Which was it?'

'Breckinridge is his name.'

'Ah! I don't know him. Well, here's your good health, landlord, and prosperity to your house. Good-night.'

'Now for Mr Breckinridge,' he continued, buttoning up his coat, as we came out into the frosty air. 'Remember, Watson, that though we have so homely a thing as a goose at one end of this chain, we have at the other a man who will certainly get seven years' penal servitude, unless we can establish his innocence. It is possible that our inquiry may but confirm his guilt; but, in any case, we have a line of investigation which has been missed by the police, and which a singular chance has placed in our hands. Let us follow it out to the bitter end. Faces to the south, then, and quick march!'

We passed across Holborn, down Endell-street, and so through a zigzag of slums to Covent Garden Market. One of the largest stalls bore the name of Breckinridge upon it, and the proprietor, a horsey-looking man, with a sharp face and trim side-whiskers, was helping a boy to put up the shutters.

'Good evening. It's a cold night,' said Holmes.

The salesman nodded, and shot a questioning glance at my companion. 'Sold out of geese, I see,' continued Holmes, pointing at the bare slabs of marble.

'Let you have five hundred tomorrow morning.'

'That's no good.'

'Well, there are some on the stall with the gas flare.'

'Ah, but I was recommended to you.'

'Who by?'

'The landlord of the "Alpha".'

'Oh, yes; I sent him a couple of dozen.'

'Fine birds they were, too. Now where did you get them from?'

To my surprise the question provoked a burst of anger from the sales man.

'Now, then, mister,' said he, with his head cocked and his arms akimbo, 'what are you driving at? Let's have it straight, now.'

'It is straight enough. I should like to know who sold you the geese which you supplied to the "Alpha".'

'Well, then, I sh'an't tell you. So now!'

'Oh, it is a matter of no importance; but I don't know why you should be so warm over such a trifle.'

'Warm! You'd be as warm, maybe, if you were as pestered as I am. When I pay good money for a good article there should be an end of the business; but it's "Where are the geese?" and "Who did you sell the geese to?" and "What will you take for the geese?" One would think they were the only geese in the world, to hear the fuss that is made over them.'

'Well, I have no connection with any other people who have been making inquiries,' said Holmes carelessly. 'If you won't tell us the bet is off, that is all. But I'm always ready to back my opinion on a matter of fowls, and I have a fiver on it that the bird I ate is country bred.'

'Well, then, you've lost your fiver, for it's town bred,' snapped the salesman.

'It's nothing of the kind.'

'I say it is.'

'I don't believe it.'

'D'you think you know more about fowls than I, who have handled them ever since I was a nipper? I tell you, all those birds that went to the "Alpha" were town bred.'

'You'll never persuade me to believe that.'

'Will you bet, then?'

'It's merely taking your money, for I know that I am right. But I'll have a sovereign on with you, just to teach you not to be obstinate.'

The salesman chuckled grimly. 'Bring me the books, Bill,' said he.

The small boy brought round a small thin volume and a great greasy-backed one, laying them out together beneath the hanging lamp.

'Now then, Mr Cocksure,' said the salesman, 'I thought that I was out of geese, but before I finish you'll find that there is still one left in my shop. You see this little book?'

'Well?'

'That's the list of the folk from whom I buy. D'you see? Well, then, here on this page are the country folk, and the numbers after their names are where their accounts are in the big ledger. Now, then! You see this other page in red ink? Well, that is a list of my town suppliers. Now, look at that third name. Just read it out to me.'

'"Mrs Oakshott, 117, Brixton-road – 249,"' read Holmes.

'Quite so. Now turn that up in the ledger.'

Holmes turned to the page indicated. 'Here you are, "Mrs Oakshott, 117, Brixton-road, egg and poultry supplier."'

'Now, then, what's the last entry?'

"December 22. Twenty-four geese at 7s. 6d."

'Quite so. There you are. And underneath?'

'"Sold to Mr Windigate of the 'Alpha' at 12s."'

'What have you to say now?'

Sherlock Holmes looked deeply chagrined. He drew a sovereign from his pocket and threw it down upon the slab, turning away with the air of a man whose disgust is too deep for words. A few yards off he stopped under a lamp-post, and laughed in the hearty, noiseless fashion which was peculiar to him.

'When you see a man with whiskers of that cut and the "pink 'un" protruding out of his pocket, you can always draw him by a bet,' said he. 'I daresay that if I had put a hundred pounds down in front of him that man would not have given me such complete information as was drawn from him by the idea that he was doing me on a wager. Well, Watson, we are, I fancy, nearing the end of our quest, and the only point which remains to be determined is whether we should go on to this Mrs Oakshott tonight, or whether we should reserve it for tomorrow. It is clear from what that surly fellow said that there are others besides ourselves who are anxious about the matter, and I should –'

His remarks were suddenly cut short by a loud hubbub which broke out from the stall which we had just left. Turning round we saw a little rat-faced fellow standing in the centre of the circle of yellow light which was thrown by the swinging lamp, while Breckinridge the salesman, framed in the door of his stall, was shaking his fists fiercely at the cringing figure.

'I've had enough of you and your geese,' he shouted. 'I wish you were all at the devil together. If you come pestering me any more with your silly talk I'll set the dog at you. You bring Mrs Oakshott here and I'll answer her, but what have you to do with it? Did I buy the geese off you?'

'No; but one of them was mine all the same,' whined the little man.

'Well, then, ask Mrs Oakshott for it.'

'She told me to ask you.'

'Well, you can ask the King of Proosia for all I care. I've had enough of it. Get out of this!' He rushed fiercely forward, and the inquirer flitted away into the darkness.

'Ha, this may save us a visit to Brixton-road,' whispered Holmes. 'Come with me, and we will see what is to be made of this fellow.' Striding through the scattered knots of people who lounged round the flaring stalls, my companion speedily overtook the little man and touched him upon the shoulder. He sprang round, and I could see in the gaslight that every vestige of colour had been driven from his face.

'Who are you, then? What do you want?' he asked in a quavering voice.

'You will excuse me,' said Holmes, blandly, 'but I could not help overhearing the questions which you put to the salesman just now. I think that I could be of assistance to you.'

'You? Who are you? How could you know anything of the matter?'

'My name is Sherlock Holmes. It is my business to know what other people don't know.'

'But you can know nothing of this?'

'Excuse me, I know everything of it. You are endeavouring to trace some geese which were sold by Mrs Oakshott, of Brixton-road, to a salesman named Breckinridge, by him in turn to Mr Windigate, of the "Alpha", and by him to his club, of which Mr Henry Baker is a member.'

'Oh, sir, you are the very man whom I have longed to meet,' cried the little fellow, with outstretched hands and quivering fingers. 'I can hardly explain to you how interested I am in this matter.'

Sherlock Holmes hailed a four-wheeler which was passing. 'In that case we had better discuss it in a cosy room rather than in this windswept market-place,' said he. 'But pray tell me, before we go further, who it is that I have the pleasure of assisting.'

The man hesitated for an instant. 'My name is John Robinson,' he answered, with a sidelong glance.

'No, no; the real name,' said Holmes, sweetly. 'It is always awkward doing business with an *alias*.'

A flush sprang to the white cheeks of the stranger. 'Well, then,' said he, 'my real name is James Ryder.'

'Precisely so. Head attendant at the Hotel Cosmopolitan. Pray step into the cab, and I shall soon be able to tell you everything which you would wish to know.'

The little man stood glancing from one to the other of us with half-frightened, half-hopeful eyes, as one who is not sure whether he is on the verge of a windfall or of a catastrophe. Then he stepped into the cab, and in half an hour we were back in the sitting-room at Baker-street. Nothing had been said during our drive, but the high, thin breathing of our new companion, and the claspings and unclaspings of his hands, spoke of the nervous tension within him.

'Here we are!' said Holmes, cheerily, as we filed into the room. 'The fire looks very seasonable in this weather. You look cold, Mr Ryder. Pray take the basket chair. I will just put on my slippers before we settle this little matter of yours. Now, then! You want to know what became of those geese?'

'Yes, sir.'

'Or rather, I fancy, of that goose. It was one bird, I imagine, in which you were interested – white, with a black bar across the tail.'

Ryder quivered with emotion. 'Oh, sir,' he cried, 'can you tell me where it went to.'

'It came here.'

'Here?'

'Yes, and a most remarkable bird it proved. I don't wonder that you should take an interest in it. It laid an egg after it was dead – the bonniest, brightest little blue egg that ever was seen. I have it here in my museum.'

Our visitor staggered to his feet, and clutched the mantelpiece with his right hand. Holmes unlocked his strong box, and held up the blue carbuncle, which shone out like a star, with a cold, brilliant, many-pointed radiance. Ryder stood glaring with a drawn face, uncertain whether to claim or to disown it.

'The game's up, Ryder,' said Holmes, quietly. 'Hold up, man, or you'll be into the fire. Give him an arm back into his chair, Watson. He's not got blood enough to go in for felony with impunity. Give him a dash of brandy. So! Now he looks a little more human. What a shrimp it is, to be sure!'

For a moment he had staggered and nearly fallen, but the brandy brought a tinge of colour into his cheeks, and he sat staring with frightened eyes at his accuser.

'I have almost every link in my hands, and all the proofs which I could possibly need, so there is little which you need tell me. Still that little may as well be cleared up to make the case complete. You had heard, Ryder, of this blue stone of the Countess of Morcar's?'

'It was Catherine Cusack who told me of it,' said he, in a crackling voice.

'I see. Her ladyship's waiting-maid. Well, the temptation of sudden wealth so easily acquired was too much for you, as it has been for better men before you; but you were not very scrupulous in the means you used. It seems to me, Ryder, that there is the making of a very pretty villain in you. You knew that this man Horner, the plumber, had been concerned in some such matter before, and that suspicion would rest the more readily upon him. What did you do, then? You made some small job in my lady's room – you and your confederate Cusack – and you managed that he should be the man sent for. Then, when he had left, you rifled the jewel case, raised the alarm, and had this unfortunate man arrested. You then –'

Ryder threw himself down suddenly upon the rug, and clutched at my companion's knees. 'For God's sake, have mercy!' he shrieked. 'Think of my father! Of my mother! It would break their hearts. I never went wrong before! I never will again. I swear it. I'll swear it on a Bible. Oh, don't bring it into court! For Christ's sake, don't!'

'Get back into your chair!' said Holmes, sternly. 'It is very well to cringe and crawl now, but you thought little enough of this poor Horner in the dock for a crime of which he knew nothing.'

'I will fly, Mr Holmes. I will leave the country, sir. Then the charge against him will break down.'

'Hum! We will talk about that. And now let us hear a true account of the next act. How came the stone into the goose, and how came the goose into the open market? Tell us the truth, for there lies your only hope of safety.'

Ryder passed his tongue over his parched lips. 'I will tell you it just as it happened, sir,' said he. 'When Horner had been arrested, it seemed to me that it would be best for me to get away with the stone at once, for I did not know at what moment the police might not take it into their heads to search me and my room. There was no place about the hotel where it would be safe. I went out, as if on some commission, and I made for my sister's house. She had married a man named Oakshott, and lived in Brixton-road, where she fattened fowls for the market. All the way there every man I met seemed to me to be a policeman or a detective, and for all that it was a cold night, the sweat was pouring down my face before I came to the Brixton-road. My sister asked me what was the matter, and why I was so pale; but I told her that I had been upset by the jewel robbery at the hotel. Then I went into the back yard, and smoked a pipe, and wondered what it would be best to do.

'I had a friend once called Maudsley, who went to the bad, and has just been serving his time in Pentonville. One day he had met me, and fell into talk about the ways of thieves and how they could get rid of what they stole. I knew that he would be true to me, for I knew one or two things about him, so I made up my mind to go right on to Kilburn, where he lived, and take him into my confidence. He would show me how to turn the stone into money. But how to get to him in safety. I thought of the agonies I had gone through in coming from the hotel. I might at any moment be seized and searched, and there would be the stone in my waistcoat pocket. I was leaning against the

wall at the time, and looking at the geese which were wad-
dling about round my feet, and suddenly an idea came
into my head which showed me how I could beat the best
detective that ever lived.

'My sister had told me some weeks before that I might
have the pick of her geese for a Christmas present, and I
knew that she was always as good as her word. I would
take my goose now, and in it I would carry my stone to
Kilburn. There was a little shed in the yard, and behind
this I drove one of the birds, a fine big one, white with a
barred tail. I caught it, and, prising its bill open, I thrust
the stone down its throat as far as my finger could reach.
The bird gave a gulp, and I felt the stone pass along its
gullet and down into its crop. But the creature flapped
and struggled, and out came my sister to know what was
the matter. As I turned to speak to her the brute broke
loose, and fluttered off among the others.

'"Whatever were you doing with that bird, Jem?" says she.

'"Well," said I, "you said you'd give me one for Christmas, and I was feeling which was the fattest."

'"Oh," says she, "we've set yours aside for you. Jem's
bird, we call it. It's the big, white one over yonder. There's
twenty-six of them, which makes one for you, and one for
us, and two dozen for the market."

'"Thank you, Maggie," says I; "but if it is all the same
to you I'd rather have that one I was handling just now."

'"The other is a good three pound heavier," she said,
"and we fattened it expressly for you."

'"Never mind. I'll have the other, and I'll take it now," said I.

'"Oh, just as you like," said she, a little huffed. "Which is it you want, then?"

'"That white one, with the barred tail, right in the middle of the flock."

'"Oh, very well. Kill it and take it with you."

'"Well, I did what she said, Mr Holmes, and I carried the bird all the way to Kilburn. I told my pal what I had done, for he was a man that it was easy to tell a thing like that to. He laughed until he choked, and we got a knife and opened the goose. My heart turned to water, for there was no sign of the stone, and I knew that some terrible mistake had occurred. I left the bird, rushed back to my sister's, and hurried into the back yard. There was not a bird to be seen there.

'"Where are they all, Maggie?" I cried.

'"Gone to the dealer's."

'"Which dealer's?"

'"Breckinridge, of Covent Garden.'

'"But was there another with a barred tail?" I asked, "the same as the one I chose?"

' "Yes, Jem, there were two barred-tailed ones, and I could never tell them apart."

'Well, then, of course, I saw it all, and I ran off as hard as my feet would carry me to this man Breckinridge; but he had sold the lot at once, and not one word would he tell me as to where they had gone. You heard him yourselves tonight. Well, he has always answered me like that. My sister thinks that I am going mad. Sometimes I think that I am myself. And now – and now I am myself a branded thief, without ever having touched the wealth for which I sold my character. God help me! God help me!' He burst into convulsive sobbing, with his face buried in his hands.

There was a long silence, broken only by his heavy breathing, and by the measured tapping of Sherlock Holmes' finger-tips upon the edge of the table. Then my friend rose, and threw open the door.

'Get out!' said he.

'What, sir! Oh, heaven bless you!'

'No more words. Get out!'

And no more words were needed. There was a rush, a clatter upon the stairs, the bang of a door, and the crisp rattle of running footfalls from the street.

'After all, Watson,' said Holmes, reaching up his hand for his clay pipe, 'I am not retained by the police to supply their deficiencies. If Horner were in danger it would be another thing, but this fellow will not appear against him, and the case must collapse. I suppose that I am commuting a felony, but it is just possible that I am saving a soul. This fellow will not go wrong again. He is too terribly frightened. Send him to gaol now, and you make him a gaol-bird for life. Besides, it is the season of forgiveness. Chance has put in our way a most singular and whimsical problem, and its solution is its own reward. If you will have the goodness to touch the bell, Doctor, we will begin another investigation, in which also a bird will be the chief feature.'

ACKNOWLEDGEMENTS

Every effort has been made to trace and contact all copyright holders. If there are any inadvertent omissions or errors we will be pleased to correct them at the earliest opportunity.

Vintage Classics gratefully acknowledges permission to reprint copyright material as follows:

Raymond Carver: 'A Serious Talk' from *What We Talk About When We Talk About Love* (1938) by Raymond Carver. Copyright © 1981 By Raymond Carver. First published in Great Britain by The Harvill Press. Reprinted by permission of The Random House Group Limited in the UK, and by permission of Alfred A. Knopf, an imprint of the Knopf Doubleday Publishing Group, a division of Penguin Random House LLC. All rights reserved. Any third party use of this material, outside of this publication, is

Stella Gibbons: 'Christmas at Cold Comfort Farm' from *Christmas at Cold Comfort Farm* (1940) by Stella Gibbons. Copyright © Stella Gibbons 1940. Reproduced with permission of Curtis Brown Group Ltd, London on behalf of The Estate of Stella Gibbons.

Laurie Lee: 'Carol-Barking', extract from *Cider with Rosie* by Laurie Lee (1959). Copyright © Laurie Lee 1959. First published by Hogarth Press. Reprinted by permission of The Random House Group Limited.

Alice Munro: 'The Turkey Season' from *The Moons of Jupites* by Alice Munro. Copyright © Alice Munro 1977, 1978, 1979, 1980, 1981, 1982. Used by permission of Alfred A. Knopf, an imprint of the Knopf Doubleday Publishing Group, a division of Penguin Random House LLC. All rights reserved.

Helen Simpson: 'Let Nothing You Dismay' from *Dear George and Other Stories* (1995) by Helen Simpson. Copyright © Helen Simpson 1995. First published by William Heinemann. Reprinted by permission of The Random House Group Limited.

How do we survive Christmas?

Drinking
JOHN CHEEVER

VINTAGE MINIS

Love
JEANETTE WINTERSON

VINTAGE MINIS

Eating
NIGELLA LAWSON

VINTAGE MINIS

Calm
TIM PARKS

VINTAGE MINIS

VINTAGE MINIS

The Vintage Minis bring you some of the world's greatest writers on the experiences that make us human. These stylish, entertaining little books explore the whole spectrum of life – from birth to death, and everything in between. Which means there's something here for everyone, whatever your story.

vintageminis.co.uk